ALL - BRIGHT COURT

ALL-BRIGHT COURT

CONNIE PORTER

HOUGHTON MIFFLIN COMPANY

BOSTON 1991

For information about permission to reproduce selections from
this book, write to Permissions, Houghton Mifflin Company,
2 Park Street, Boston, Massachusetts 02108.

Library of Congress Cataloging-in-Publication Data

Porter, Connie Rose, date.
All-Bright Court / Connie Porter.
p.   cm.
ISBN 0-395-53271-X
I. Title.
PS3566.06424A74   1991   91-8105
813'.54—dc20   CIP

Printed in the United States of America

AGM 10 9 8 7 6 5 4 3 2 1

The chapter "Hoodoo" has appeared in different form in *The Southern
Review* and in *Breaking Ice: An Anthology of Contemporary African
American Fiction,* edited by Terry McMillan (Viking Press, 1990).

For Mama and Malcolm

ACKNOWLEDGMENTS

I want to thank everyone whose support and understanding I've had over the years: my eight brothers and sisters and the rest of my family; Mrs. Gist, Mrs. Drajem, and Mr. Soffin; Moira and Rodger for believing in me when I didn't believe in myself; and Freddie for his help. Thanks to Milton Academy for giving me the time and space to write this book, and to Lisa and Sid for *Seboyokani*. Above all, thank you Lynne, Ellen, Janet, and Larry. Without you this book would still be a dream.

ALL-BRIGHT COURT

1

ALIGHTING

AT EIGHT in the morning Samuel Taylor was eating eggs. There were three of them, sunny-side up, the yolks softly set. He had cut them up, and when he slid pieces of the slick whites into his mouth, yolk ran down his chin. He was making a mess, but he did not care. All the men, the steelworkers, who came to Dulski's ate like this. They were not kind to food. They sat at the counter, grunting, slurping, talking.

On the wall behind the counter was a sign: NO CREDIT, DON'T ASK! A frame containing a one dollar bill was next to it. Underneath the frame was a picture of Dulski on the day he opened the diner. He was holding the bill that was now framed. None of the men quite knew when the diner had opened. It seemed as if it had always been there, hunched in the shadow of Capital Steel. Dulski still looked the same. But the men joked that if you looked close enough at the picture, you could see that the eagle on the back of the bill was still inside its egg.

The years of frying had left a permanent film of grease on

everything in the diner. At least once a year the stove caught fire, and one or two of the men seated at the counter had to help douse it. No one would have been surprised to show up at the diner on any day and find it had burned down.

But the men kept coming. Though Dulski's smelled of rancid tallow, old fried onions, stale cigar and cigarette smoke, it was a place to alight, to stop on the way home or to work. Samuel still stopped in out of habit on his way back to All-Bright Court at the end of his shift.

As Samuel sat at the counter, a group of men came in, black men and white men. They came to Dulski's for breakfast and coffee and talk before they went home to their separate worlds. As they stomped through Dulski's door, they brought in with them the cold and snow swirling softly outside.

"Kennedy's going to take the election," one of the men was saying.

"I don't know," another said. "The union's talking about backing Nixon."

"Nixon, that bum!"

"That bum got us out of the strike last year."

"Get outta here. The U.S.W. can back who it wants. It's Democrat all the way for me, and Kennedy's going to take it."

"Hell, if they let them vote for him in Canada, he'll take that too."

"We're going to put him in, and then we're never going to let him forget it."

All of the men laughed.

"Damn right. He'll owe us."

"Bullshit," a wheezy voice called out, and the men became quiet. "The U.A.W. is going to put him in. That's where the power is," the voice said, breaking into a barking laugh.

"Yeah, but where would the U.A.W. be without the U.S.W.A." It was a statement, not a question. "It's the U.S.W.A. This country would be nothing without us, the brotherhood."

"Yeah, the brotherhood."

"Damn straight."

Samuel Taylor had first come into Dulski's two years earlier, fresh from Tupelo. He'd stood out front on the sidewalk, staring through the window in disbelief. Black men were sitting at the counter elbow to elbow with white men. They were all eating.

Just seeing the men had stopped Samuel cold, left him fluttering just outside the door, hesitant to enter, until one of the white men waved at him, inviting him in. Back home this would never have happened. Black and white men did not eat together, not there, not then.

They had not eaten together at the lunch counter in the five-and-dime where Samuel had washed dishes after he dropped out of high school.

He was a boy then. Both of his parents were dead. When Samuel was ten, his father had been struck and killed by a hit-and-run driver. Five years later his mother died, he wasn't sure why. All he knew was that she had female trouble, and she spent the last month of her life in bed, moaning like a ghost. Her sister tended to her. After his mother died, Samuel and his older brother went to live with their mother's sister and her husband.

"I'm not feeding ya'll" was the first thing the uncle said when the boys moved in. "We done raised our own, and I don't want you here."

The aunt shooed the boys into the back room, which was dark and smelled of kerosene. "He drinking. Don't pay him no mind."

The uncle meant what he said. The aunt fed them out of the money she earned as a domestic. She usually was not home at dinner, but she left a pot of beans or greens on the stove for the boys.

One night when Samuel's brother came home from shining shoes, he found that Samuel had already served himself from the pot. The brother looked into the pot on the stove, then into Samuel's bowl. Without saying a word, he punched Samuel in the face. He hit Samuel so hard that he knocked him off his chair.

"Who you think you is? Taking all the meat." He reached into Samuel's bowl and took Samuel's piece of fatback.

Samuel did not say anything. He lay on the floor, his nose bloody, his lip cut.

When he awoke the next morning, he found a quarter by his pillow.

Within the week his brother was gone.

"That make one less mouth for me to feed," the uncle said. "All we got to do is get rid of you," he added, nodding his head toward Samuel.

Samuel hated his brother, not for leaving, but for leaving him behind.

He did not know if his brother had gone north or if he had gone into the fields and sold his future for a handful of seeds. Young as he was, Samuel knew he would not trade in his dreams for cottonseed, dry and hard and borrowed. He would go north when he was older. It did not matter where.

Samuel knew what he knew of the North from men who had never traveled beyond the boundaries of their dusty towns, men who had spent their days sharecropping, bent over in fields of cotton. These men claimed word came to them from those who had gone. A brother, an uncle, a neighbor, a friend's third cousin.

It was true, word sometimes came, but more often they created it. As the men worked stooped in the fields, they changed the dirt that passed through their hands into flesh, breathed life into it, and proclaimed its truth.

"A colored man up north live like a king. My cousin live in Chicago, in a brick tower. Got running water. Gas heat."

"I knows a man what buy a new car every year."

"I'm a go north one day," someone would invariably add.

But one day never came for these men. They did not have one day to call their own, not yesterday, today, or tomorrow. They had borrowed against all the days of all their lives, and it seemed that even in death they worked in the blue haze of night, rising from the earth, their sacks on their backs, picking until dawn, until the light of day pushed them back into the ground.

If Samuel was going to escape their fate and make it north, he would need more than borrowed seeds. He would need money. He stopped going to school and began walking the streets of Tupelo looking for a job.

It was nearly a month before he found one, washing dishes at the five-and-dime.

Samuel had walked past the store before and had seen white people eating, sipping pastel shakes from tall glasses, artificial light bouncing off the counter, giving everything a heavenly glow. He had gone into the store only once before. When the quarter had materialized, he had gone in to buy candy.

It had been lunchtime. The stainless-steel counter stretched almost the entire length of the store. It ran right up to the front window, ending in a graceful curve. The stools were stainless also, topped with red padded cushions. On the wall behind the counter were pictures of meat loaf platters, burgers and fries, slices of pie, shakes. Each picture had the price of the item written in a circle in the lower right corner.

There was a picture of a banana split, and in its circle was the price. Twenty-five cents.

Samuel had stood mesmerized, the warm quarter closed in his hand. A string of saliva dripped from his mouth and onto the polished tile floor. It broke his trance, and he quickly turned from the counter. He was going crazy. Thinking of sitting on a stool. Thinking that he had the right to eat there in the splendor and glow of the counter. He still wanted to buy the candy, but he did not know where to find it. Instead of looking for it, he left the store, went to the grocer, and bought sardines and crackers.

But the scene at the counter, its shining splendor, stayed in his mind, and he found himself in front of the store again a month later. As he stood there on the sidewalk he saw a black man wearing a white uniform turn into the narrow alley between the five-and-dime and the drugstore. Samuel followed him, and to his surprise the man turned to him. "They hiring," the man said.

Five black men worked in the kitchen. Four cooked, and one did the dishes. The manager, a young white man with a red butch, supervised them, and four white waitresses worked out front. Samuel was taken on as a second dish-washer. In addition to washing dishes, he swept, mopped, and put out the garbage.

He was a clumsy boy, breaking dishes, slipping and falling on the greasy floor. The men laughed at him. One of them, a cook with two gold front teeth, said, "You one of them boys going to follow the drinking gourd. I can tell you got your eyes turned north."

"Yes, sir," Samuel said, surprised and pleased that some-one had taken notice of him. "I'm a be going north soon's I can."

"Boys like you be coming in here all the time. But let me tell you something. The way you be working, you liable not to make enough money to cross the street."

"Sir?" Samuel said. He was annoyed.

"Boy, keep your mind on your work. Watch what you doing, 'cause if you keep on this way, the closest you going to get to the North is in your dreams."

Samuel did not say anything, and he became more mindful of his tasks, but he decided he did not like this cook. Who was he, anyway, and what did he know?

But each day the golden-tooth cook, whose name was Parker Bell, would have a plate of food waiting for Samuel at the end of the day, after he finished cleaning. Parker made meals the likes of which Samuel had never seen. Each meal was a Sunday dinner, fried chicken, liver and onions, smothered pork chops. Samuel would reluctantly accept the platters Parker put before him. Though he ate from the same white plates the customers at the gleaming counter ate from, he ate standing by the sink in the kitchen, devouring his food like a starving animal.

One evening after everyone else was gone, Parker said, "Don't eat standing up. Food go right to your feet that way. Don't you know that?"

"Naw," Samuel said, his mouth stuffed with mashed potatoes.

"I believe you don't. You act like a boy ain't got nobody to learn you nothing. You a boy ain't got nobody to learn you nothing?"

Samuel glared at him. "You the one don't know nothing. I know enough to leave here. You won't catch me standing in no kitchen when I'm a grown man."

"Let me tell you something," Parker said. "You don't know your ass from your elbow. I ain't got to cook for you, boy. But I see you come here, a raggedy-ass boy, raggedy as a bowl of sauerkraut. I see you boys coming in here. Dreaming. Dreaming. Them *my* dreams ya'll got in ya'll eyes. Ya'll daddy's dreams. Ya'll grandaddy's.

"We ain't made it. I ain't going to make it. Look 'round here," Parker said, waving a spatula. "This my life, boy. This how big it's ever going be. And let me tell you something. I chastise you 'cause I'm trying to teach you something. Think ya'll got dreams men my age ain't never had." Parker took off his apron and folded it.

A biscuit was swelling in Samuel's mouth. He watched Parker put on a thin cotton jacket.

"Put the light out when you finish, boy."

Samuel forced himself to swallow the pasty biscuit. He scraped the food left on his plate into the garbage can and washed his plate and fork.

When he went home, the uncle was sitting in the living room in the dark, listening to the radio. "Your aunt sleeping at work tonight. She be back tomorrow night," he said.

Samuel stood staring at him, his figure, the hole it punched in the darkness.

"What you looking at, boy?" the shadow asked.

"Nothing," Samuel said, and he went to his room and wept.

The next evening at work Samuel stood over the sink trying to finish up rapidly. He had not been able to bring himself to look at Parker all day. But when he was getting down to the last few pots, a hand slid a plate of food onto the drain board.

"Thank you," he said softly. He dried his hands on his apron, pulled up a stool, and sat down.

"That's better," Parker said. "Since you know how to sit down and eat, I might can have you over to the house sometime."

Parker invited him the next week, to church and Sunday

dinner. Samuel had one suit of Sunday clothes, the one he had worn to his mother's funeral. When he tried it on, he discovered it had shrunk. The pants and jacket were both too short. The jacket was too tight across the chest, and he could not get the pants zipped. He had his own money, so he dipped into his savings to buy a pair of pants, a new shirt, a new pair of shoes, all of which were too big.

Parker waited until dinner to comment on Samuel's clothes. "Let me tell you something, Sam. A colored man in the South got to know how big he is."

"That ain't right," Parker's daughter said. Her name was Mary Kate. She was a girl with skin as shiny and black and purple as eggplant. "It ain't right," she repeated, her voice rising. "We can't even try on clothes."

Samuel sat staring at her. The gold in Parker's mouth was not his only wealth.

"In the North a colored man ain't got to know his size. In the North a man can be as big as he want," Parker said.

"I hear you going north," Parker's wife said.

"Yes, ma'am," Samuel said.

"What your mama think? You still a young boy."

"I don't have no mama. No daddy neither," Samuel said flatly.

"I'm sorry to hear that," Parker's wife said.

"I'm going north too," Mary Kate interjected. Samuel looked at her and smiled. He was picking at his food.

"What's wrong with the food?" Parker asked.

"Nothing. It's real good."

"Well eat up, boy," Parker said.

"Parker," his wife said, "let the boy alone."

Samuel was too nervous to eat. He would always believe that he had fallen in love with Mary Kate on this very first day.

"You ain't going nowhere till you finish high school," Parker said to Mary Kate. "And you might not go then."

"We could all go, Daddy," she said, and then turned to Samuel. "My daddy got a cousin living in Cleveland, living real good."

"Columbus," her mother said. "And don't be bragging."

"We could all go someday," Mary Kate said.

"We'll see," Parker said.

Samuel began coming over to Parker's every weekend. For nearly two years he would come by on Saturdays and take Mary Kate to the movies, and he would have little gifts for her that he'd bought at the five-and-dime, candy, nuts, satin flowers, perfume. He even brought her two goldfish once. Mary Kate placed them in a shallow bowl on her bedside table, but when she woke up the next morning they had disappeared. At first she thought maybe they had turned themselves into birds and flown away. But when her feet touched the ground she saw them lying on the floor looking wide-eyed and surprised.

On Sundays Samuel and Mary Kate would go to church with her parents, and then have dinner. He first kissed her on a Sunday. They were hidden in the canopy of a peach tree in her back yard, supposedly picking peaches. Surrounded by the dark greenness, he discovered the insides of her cheeks were like cantaloupe, wet and soft and slick.

Parker knew the time had come for Samuel to leave, and as they were finishing up work one evening he said, "You slowing up."

"No, sir," Samuel said. "I'm the fastest dishwasher in Tupelo."

"Yeah, and if you keep it up, you can say that for a lifetime. I ain't talking 'bout your work, son. You sweet on my daughter, and she slowing you up."

"She not slowing me up. I'm not slowing . . . What's wrong with me liking her?"

"Ain't a thing wrong with it. Let me tell you something. If I thought something was wrong with it, you wouldn't be seeing her."

"You think I ain't going north," Samuel said.

"Let me tell you something. There's another boy that like Mary Kate."

"Who?" Samuel asked, his voice filled with anger. "She ain't never said nothing 'bout a boy."

"Women don't never tell you they seeing somebody else. What, you crazy, boy? Women smart. But don't you get riled up. She ain't stutting him, and he got a college education. This boy went to Southern. You know Southern?"

"No," Samuel said, disgusted. He wiped white suds from his hands and sat down.

"It's a Negro college in Baton Rouge. Boy got him a degree. And you know what he do?"

Samuel did not answer.

"I say, you know what he do?"

"No," Samuel said.

"He a Pullman porter, riding the Crescent from New Orleans to Chicago. Up and down. Back and forth. Come here time to time talking big. He fenna move to Chicago. He fenna get him a job up in a skyscraper. Going to sit on top the world. Only thing, that he stuck on the train. I think the boy scared to get off up there."

"You don't think I can make it up north," Samuel said.

"I ain't say that."

"You say this college boy ain't make it," Samuel said.

"I say this college boy ain't make it. Get the potatoes out your ears, boy. I say he too scared to try. Don't get me wrong now. I ain't knocking a education. A education a good thing. I wish I had one, a piece of paper saying I was smart. But a piece of paper don't make you a man. That boy don't think he a man. You think you a man, I know that. Necking with my daughter."

Samuel smiled, his eyes cast down.

"You think you a damn grown man. I'm telling you it's time to go. You letting your dreams slip through your fingers a nickel at a time. You got to go and do what you got to do. Mary Kate ain't going nowhere. You make good up north, and you can come back for her," Parker said.

Samuel had made good. He'd gone to New York, upstate, where the steel mills were hiring. He had gotten a job at Capital Steel, saved his money, and two years later he married Mary Kate and brought her back to Lackawanna, a small city just south of Buffalo.

The day she arrived, he paraded her up and down the main street of the town, Ridge Road, as if the three blocks were the Great White Way. There was a five-and-dime, a cleaners, a laundry, churches, an A & P. The grocery store was huge — eight aisles, six check-out counters. The smell of freshly ground coffee filled the store. Sawdust was sprinkled on the polished wooden floor. A red-faced butcher stood behind the meat counter.

They went to the Jubilee Theatre and sat in the front row. They had ice cream sodas at the counter in the drugstore. They even went skating. But Mary Kate didn't want to go to Dulski's Diner. "I can cook at home," Mary Kate would say. Home for them was 18 All-Bright Court.

Samuel sopped up the eggs that had dripped onto his plate with a piece of white bread, quickly finished his coffee, and put some change on the counter. The snow bit at his face as he left the steamy warmth of the diner and hurried back to All-Bright Court, his hand-me-down home.

Capital Steel had thrown the tenement together during World War I in an effort to bury the Germans, two hundred units of nameless temporary housing built in the shadow of the plant for the white workers — the Poles, the Italians, the Slavs, even the Germans — who showed up day after day like migrating birds. Even as the cinder blocks of the buildings were being set in place they were crumbling. It made no difference to the men who moved in with their families. They arrived with their bellies empty and their mouths full of lies. They showed up daily, lying in Polish, in Italian, in Russian, and even in German, saying they knew how to work steel, knew about coke ovens and blast furnaces, rolling mills. What great liars they were; they knew telling the truth was a guarantee of nothing. This was the first chance many of them had had to live on their own. They moved their families out of drafty boarding houses, out of a brother's, an in-law's, a cousin's, a friend's. It meant a front and back yard, a stone front porch that was shared with a neighbor, a back stoop of their own, an upstairs and downstairs. Thirteen rectangular buildings stood on one side of Hanna, a dead-end street; on the other were twelve. Each building contained eight two-story apartments, all facing west to east, their backs to the sun.

Day and night the men went to work from their temporary housing. The women stayed home and watched clouds of red, gray, and orange smoke scudding across the hazy sky. Their men made these clouds. Night and day. More than five thousand men worked at the plant, worked day and night. They were an army; it was they who buried the Germans.

Twenty-five years later they buried the Germans again. They were an even bigger army now. Ten thousand men descending into the mouth of hell, night and day.

The tenement was still there, falling apart, its cinders turning into ashes. Capital promised to build the men new homes. Some men didn't wait. They began building houses on the streets surrounding the tenement, staking claim to their futures with thirty-year mortgages.

It was not until 1955 that Capital built new houses for the workers, five hundred houses in Capital Park, a town just to the south of Lackawanna, and five hundred more in a section of Lackawanna across the tracks it named Capital Heights. These prefab houses, trucked in and assembled on half-acre lots, were built for the Poles, the Russians, the Serbs, the Czechs, the Yugoslavs, the Romanians, the English, the Irish, the Scots, the Danes, the Italians, and even the Germans.

No blacks were permitted to buy the houses. Capital was not being unfair, but the past could not be changed.

So the buildings of the tenement were painted to stop them from crumbling, and they were handed down to the black workers. The buildings were painted bright colors, blue, white, yellow, pink, green, and the tenement was given a name, All-Bright Court. That was what it was, a reflection of postwar optimism, bright and shining.

Like Samuel, most of the people in All-Bright Court had recently come from the South, seduced by the indoor plumbing, the gas stoves, the electric refrigerators, dazzled by the splendor, the brightness of it all. Just like the white men, the black workers had mouths full of lies, though some had really worked steel before, in Birmingham, Baltimore, Pittsburgh. What they saw in All-Bright Court was the dream they dreamed down south. They did not see the promise of a dream crumbling under a few layers of paint.

2

TROUBLE

"THERE SOMETHING wrong with old-man children. They slow or they crazy. Men always blame it on the women. Say old women have 'flicted kids. But old men be having them too. It's them old sperm." This was what people said of Isaac's father. He was an old man, and Isaac looked like an old man's child.

Isaac's head was too big for his body. It was too long and thin. His hair was sparse and dry, and Dixie Peach added no sheen. The pomade made his head shine, but his hair stayed dull.

But the boy was not slow. Just as Miss Ophelia had predicted, the boy was crazy. Ten years ago, when Isaac wasn't quite two, Miss Ophelia heard him talking, talking in full sentences to his father, who was an old man even then.

"Daddy," he said. "Daddy, I'm wet. Take me home and change my diaper."

Miss Ophelia called Isaac and his father over to her porch. "That boy too little to be talking like that. He got too much sense. He using it all up now, and when he grow up he ain't going have none. You mark my words. He going to be crazy when he grow up."

Isaac pulled on his father's hand as Miss Ophelia spoke. He wanted to move on, but his father stood and listened to the woman's words. He listened out of respect because, though he was an old man, she was even older than he. When his father didn't move, Isaac let go of his father's hand and dropped to the ground. He began spinning around on his back, and when his father did not respond, he got to his knees and began banging his head on the cement. With the first hit, the skin on his forehead cracked, and blood came. His father picked him up and rushed away with Isaac in his arms. Isaac would not let his father touch his wound, so his father rubbed his legs to calm him. He found trouble hiding in the boy's legs. It was in Isaac's bones, and his father began working it out of him.

Miss Ophelia died that same year, but her words lived on as an oracle.

Over losing games of marbles or kick the can, Isaac would fall to his knees and turn his head into a hammer. He would bang it on the ground until blood pulsed out of his forehead. He banged out his thimbleful of sense into the earth. When playing red rover, the children would always dare him to come over. As he ran toward the line of intertwined arms, the children would break the chain at the last moment and let him tumble to the ground. They knew it would be a good show. They knew Isaac would bang his head, or beat on his head with his fists, or he might fall and flop around like a fish. They thought he was funny, but they also knew he was crazy. Once when he lost at mumblety-peg, he pulled his penknife from the ground and threw it at the victor.

And every time Isaac blew up, or fell out, or banged his

head on the earth, the old man soothed him with cool towels and slices of fresh orange. He pushed Isaac's mother away and rubbed trouble from his son. He worked it up from his bones. And Isaac moaned and sucked on the slices of orange as his father coaxed the trouble up through his muscles.

"It hurt, Daddy," he would say.

"I know," his father would say.

"He need his butt beat," his mother would say. "He bad."

But the other mothers on his block, and on the blocks around where he lived, did not think he was bad. They thought he was crazy.

So it was no wonder that on that August afternoon as he was running across the field along the western edge of All-Bright Court no one took notice of him and his father. No one knew this running boy was hot and mad and smelled of jute. He smelled like a bundle of wet twine. As he ran through the field of Queen Anne's lace and dandelion, he pulled the narrow blue tie from his neck and threw it in the weeds. His father was behind him. He was walking on the narrow path that had been worn through the weeds, but he couldn't keep up with Isaac. He was too old to keep up, and he had rubbed too much trouble from Isaac. He had taken on too much of his son's trouble, and it slowed him down.

"It ain't no big deal, Isaac," his father yelled. "Wait for me, son."

Isaac stood in the field wiping tears on his jacket sleeves. The tears were gone when his father caught up with him, and Isaac was making a strange moaning sound, a sound caught in his throat.

"Get up on the path, son," his father said. "I can't be walking through all them weeds. Your father is a old man."

Isaac joined his father on the path, and his father rubbed

his shoulders to release the trouble. As they walked toward home, the sound Isaac was making became louder. The moan turned back into a hollering.

"I'll buy you a bike, son," his father said. "I'll get you that English racer."

Isaac did not answer him. He knew his father couldn't afford a three-speed bike on social security. He had wanted to win the bike by becoming a paperboy for the *Buffalo Star*. He wanted to have the chance of becoming Carrier of the Month. His father had taken him on the bus to Buffalo. Isaac had dressed up in a suit and tie and gone downtown to the *Star*'s office only to be told he could not be a paperboy. He did not want to hear it. He did not want to hear, "I know we had an ad in the paper, but the *Star* does not use colored paperboys on routes that have white customers. Now if there were an all-colored route in Lackawanna, it wouldn't be a problem. That's the way business is done here. We've tried it in other neighborhoods, and there has been trouble. It's nineteen sixty. You would think we would be beyond this point. It's not my rule. I'm sorry."

Isaac did not care that the man who told him and his father this really did look sorry, that he really did sound sorry. He did not care that the man could not look at them when he said it. The man looked around his office as he spoke. He looked out his window. He couldn't look at Isaac and his father because he also had a son. He had two sons, and knew what it was a twelve-year-old boy wanted. Isaac did not care that the man shook his father's hand before they left the office. He did not know the man's hand was sweaty, that it was sweaty out of sympathy. Isaac did not know because he refused to shake the man's hand. All Isaac knew was he would not be getting an English racer.

His father was glad that Isaac had held it in so long. He

was glad Isaac was able to hold out until he had come to the field, until they were almost home.

By the time Isaac and his father had reached the end of the field, he still had not quieted. His father rubbed Isaac's shoulders until his hands hurt. That night his hands would be stiff. That night his fingers would twist into tight buds and he would not be able to open them until well after the sun rose.

As he and Isaac passed by the second row of buildings on their way back to 72, Mary Kate Taylor was in her back yard hanging clothes. Each time she bent to get another handful of pins, or to retrieve a few pieces of steaming clothes from the basket, she felt the weight of the baby she was carrying. It pulled her down, and it seemed that if she let it, it would drop her right to the center of the earth.

She could not complain, though. The baby had not kicked or stirred much. But when the old man and his son passed, the baby quickened. It moved so suddenly that she was thrown off balance. She held on to the line, and when the two had passed, when Isaac's hollering was drowned out by the roar from a smokestack at Capital, she patted her stomach.

"Don't you worry none," she said to the baby. "That ain't nothing but that old man and his crazy boy."

3

RAPTURE

IT WAS JUST before three in the afternoon and the world was ending in All-Bright Court. Venita looked out of her kitchen window, out of her yellow curtains at 92, and fell to her knees. There was a bomb, bright and hard and shining against a blue sky. The bomb was slowly moving toward her. It was stealing blood from Venita's feet. It was making her feet cold and useless.

They had finally done it. The Russians had finally dropped the bomb. It was only a matter of time. Venita had one consolation in these final few seconds of life on the planet: living in Lackawanna meant her death would be a swift and painless one.

Venita's husband, Moses, had told her, "They was worried about Florida during that missile crisis last month. But there was a real panic in Buffalo. Them Russians got it high on they list for bombing 'cause there four mills there. But it's the Capital plant they want. The biggest damn steel plant in the world. Wait till you see it. It's a monster."

Moses had told her this in the back of the Greyhound bus as they headed north four months ago. They were riding through Pennsylvania. It was the day after Thanksgiving. They had been married just two days before in Starkville, Mississippi, and were spending their honeymoon on the bus. Moses had only a week off from work, and this was already the sixth day.

"Times changing," Moses said. "The North is something else. We got whites for neighbors, got whites living on both sides of us. Polacks, the colored people be calling them. They real nice people. They speaks, and everything.

"You know, times changing all over. When I come up here in 'fifty-eight, I had to ride in the back of the bus all the way to Pennsylvania. It's just four years later, and you can set anywhere you want."

"We been riding in the back all the way now. Let's move up front," Venita said. "Let's see how things look from the front."

So Moses and Venita moved to the front of the bus and looked out the front window as snow began to fall and night began to fall, and after there was nothing left to see, they turned on the light over their seats and watched themselves watching nothing.

The next morning the bus let them off on the pike, on a day that was cold and snowless.

"There it is, baby," Moses said. "The eighth wonder of the world."

Venita was not impressed. She covered her face with both hands. "It stink," she said. "How can you stand that smell? Smell like rotten eggs."

"You get use to it," Moses said. "It don't always smell like that. Sometime it smell worser."

Moses walked his wife to their new house. He carried her

across the threshold into a house that was cold and hollow sounding.

"Welcome to Ninety All-Bright Court. This our home," he said, and placed Venita on her feet. Then he took the luggage from the porch and went upstairs while Venita looked through the kitchen.

She marveled at the mustard-colored gas stove and refrigerator. She adored the small pantry. It was already stocked with canned fruits and vegetables she had sent up. There was not a stick of furniture in the whole house. Moses wanted Venita to pick it out.

"Three rooms of furniture for two hundred ninety-nine dollars, and on time too," he had told her. They would get furniture on his first day off. But today he had to work.

Moses came downstairs, changed and ready. "I'm running late. I made a pallet on the floor upstairs, but wait up for me, hear? I be back a little after eleven," he said. "And keep the door locked, hear? You ain't in the country no more." Venita let him out the front door. She locked it behind him.

Alone in the house, Venita hung the yellow curtains she was looking out of the day the world was ending. But as she looked up through her curtains she saw the bomb disappearing. It was moving west.

As it disappeared over the top of her building, the blood returned to her feet. She could feel it return. The blood made her feet hot. Venita stood on her hot feet and moved them through the kitchen, through the living room, and out onto the front porch.

Her neighbor's boy was playing with a magnet in a patch of dirt in the front yard. Many of the children in All-Bright Court collected what they thought were pieces of the sky. They collected the silver dust that fell like rain.

It fell at three when the wind blew in from Lake Erie.

When the wind blew west over the land, the silver dust rained on All-Bright Court. It was a silver like the edges of the sky, like the bottom of the sky on sunny days.

At three, the roar came from the plant. It was the big roar of the day, like the sound of a dragon raging overhead. Underneath it the three o'clock whistle blew and five thousand men were going to work, and five thousand were going home. Inside the sound was the silver dust.

If the women looked and saw their sheets billowing away from the plant, they knew the wind was blowing from the west. Though they might not know it was the west, they knew that when the wind came from that direction it carried the silver rain. Some of them rushed to pull in their white sheets. They pulled the damp, cool sheets from the lines and took them inside to drape over the backs of kitchen chairs. Some called their children.

"Get inside this house," they would say. "Get ya'll tail in here. That dust from the plant fenna fall." And the silver came just as the women said it would. To some children it looked like glitter, and to some it looked like snow, and to some it looked like it was raining pieces of the bottom of the sky.

What was falling was iron. With magnets stolen from school, the children collected the dust, made the filings dance and snake. When the children were caught out in the silver rain, they sparkled and came home smelling base.

There was no wind on this day as Venita went to the boy dragging the magnet through the dust. She grabbed him by the shoulders. "The Russians done it, boy. The bomb, child. I saw a bomb out my back window, and it was headed this way."

The boy tried to pull away from her. "A bomb?" he asked, dropping the magnet.

She let go of his shoulders and pointed to the sky. "There

it is behind you. Look behind you, Polack boy," Venita said, and fell to her knees.

It was stealing blood from her feet again.

"We dead, boy. We going to die," she said.

The boy looked up at the sky. "I don't believe it," he said. "That's not a bomb. That's the Goodyear blimp."

4

NESTING

SAMUEL was hiding Easter eggs. Small and pastel, each was a perfect, oblong world.

Mary Kate and little Mikey had dyed them. That Samuel had refused to do. A man had to draw the line somewhere. He had drawn the line, but he still had to hide the eggs.

"If you wasn't expecting, I'd make you do this, hear?" Samuel said, smiling.

"No, you wouldn't," Mary Kate said, sitting in a chair with her feet propped up. "You ain't brought me up north to boss me."

There were only a dozen eggs, and Samuel slid them gently between the cushions of the couch, placed them carefully under the chairs, the cocktail table. He even tried to slide one under Mary Kate. "Here you go, mama hen."

"Stop playing now," she said. "You going to break it."

"Yeah," Samuel said. "You look like you going to bust, you getting so fat."

"I'm not stutting you. I'm barely pregnant. Look at you.

You getting so skinny," she said, playfully rubbing her feet across his back. "Tonight was the first time you ate good in a long while."

"We ain't going to strike. You see it in the paper? First time in nearly twenty years ain't going be a strike to get a new contract."

Mary Kate did not respond.

"We getting ten cent a hour. Don't sound like much, but it add up."

"You think he going to find 'em?" Mary Kate asked.

"What?" Samuel said.

"Do you think Mikey going to find the eggs?"

"Kate, I done left half dozen out in the middle of the floor. The boy blind if he can't see the eggs under the table."

"He only a baby."

"Come on, Kate. He just turned two his last birthday. The boy ain't stupid. Don't you think he can recognize the eggs he dyed?"

"You need to quit," Mary Kate said. "And you getting up in the morning to go on the hunt."

"The hunt? What hunt? Half the eggs out in the middle of the floor. What I look like, going on a hunt?"

"A father," Mary Kate said. "You don't never want to do these little things . . . I'm going up to bed," she said. She rose slowly from her chair and ascended the stairs.

He did not go after her, not then. He would let her be alone, let her be right.

She *was* right, but he was trying to be a man the best way he knew how. It was just like a woman to make such a fuss over eggs. Samuel provided, brought his whole check to her. He protected her too, with silence.

If he had a problem, he did not bring it home to her. What good would that do? Whatever problem he had, he held inside—even when he worried about a strike. For over a month there had been talk of a strike. Samuel had gone to Dulski's to hear what the talk was.

"This is how it's gonna be," a man with a mouthful of meat loaf yelled. "Strike!"

"We're going to bring the whole goddamn country to its knees, just like we done before."

"There won't be no strike. There's still over a month left before the contract runs out."

"That's nothing. I'll vote for a strike when the time comes."

"Jesus Christ, Dulski, watch that stove. It's flaming up there. When was the last time you cleaned it?"

"Who are you, my wife? I know what I'm doing over here."

"Strike!" someone yelled.

"Well, I'm not putting no fires out today. You're going to be on your own if that greaseball goes up."

"Strike!" Dulski screamed, branches of flames sprouting from the stove.

"Management won't jack us off."

"Union busting, that's what they're up to."

"Strike!" the man with the meat loaf in his mouth yelled.

"We'll never be beat."

"Right!"

"Right, Taylor?" a man asked Samuel. It was a man who worked at one of the coke ovens. He had eight fingers.

"Right," Samuel said. He heard his own voice, the excitement it contained. It was a voice that had conviction, a voice that believed what it said. It would rise with thousands of others in the brittle air at the lakefront. But it was also the voice of a man who was thinking how easy it would be to fly with the wind, to tuck his head and let the wind carry him south.

The men began chanting, "Strike! Strike! Strike!"

They were hypnotizing themselves, working themselves into a trance that would send them traveling back through time. They could do it like they did back in '59. One hundred and sixteen days they had held firm.

Samuel was drinking coffee and he finished quickly. It burned his mouth, and he wanted to get out, to get away from these men before his mouth said more unbelievable words. He did not want a strike, not now, not with Mary Kate having another baby. The coffee was already paid for. He had slapped down a quarter on the counter when Dulski brought the coffee to him. Now he thought of picking it up. While the men were chanting, walking through time, he could pick it up and slide it into his jacket pocket. But he did not take it. Instead, he got up from his stool and left.

Samuel walked through the snow-filled streets toward home. Mary Kate had dinner waiting for him. Pig tails. He could smell them before he opened the door, the briny smell of the vinegar she seasoned them with. He had asked her to cook them, but though he was hungry, he couldn't eat. Samuel lied. "I'm too tired to eat. I'll eat later," he said. But he didn't. He had showered at the company's Welfare Building before he left work, so he went to bed. His stomach filled with silence. If he told Mary Kate about the possibility of a strike, he would cry. He would fall into her lap and cry like a baby. What kind of man would she think he was? As it was, he was thinking that he would not be able to support her and Mikey through a prolonged strike.

When it was just him, back in '59 before Mary Kate came up, he went hungry. Even with money in the bank, with money in his pocket, he did not have enough to eat because he was saving for her to come north. He was living in a boarding house on Steelawanna then, and he had been naïve. He had never been in a strike before, and when it dragged through the early weeks, he did not worry. An event like this seemed to be contained within biblical dimensions. Forty days and forty nights. He enjoyed the time off, using it to sleep, write letters to Mary Kate, go to union meetings.

There was some kind of meeting nearly every night. The men met to celebrate their greatness. They had closed down all of the big plants, U.S. Steel, Republic, Wheeling, Allegheny. Five hundred thousand steelworkers were idle. The men had not walked out over money. All they were asking for was a seven-cent-an-hour raise over three years. They walked out over working conditions and management's claim that the union was featherbedding.

At one of the meetings a representative of local 2603 spoke. "Can you beat that? Featherbedding. We're out here working in a plant over sixty years old, and the bastards in management say we aren't efficient as the workers in plants in the Midwest. That's bullshit. It's the plants that aren't efficient. It's not us. We work like dogs," the union man yelled. "They compare our output to the output of our brothers working in plants half the age of the dinosaur we work in. They're trying to divide us. Divide and conquer. Not us. They won't divide us!"

The men jumped to their feet and applauded. Samuel jumped up with them.

The union man waved them back in their seats. His face was red, his shirt wet. "Thirty-six thousand," he said. "That's how many visits were made to the clinic last year. Thirty-six fucking thousand injuries to men in our locals, the two thousand six hundred and one, the two, the three. I don't have to tell you who you are. You had the sprained backs, the broken arms, the infected lungs, the burns. You heard of our brother in Pittsburgh, burned to death when his cherry picker fell into the candy kitchen. He was doing his job, just lifting off the lid when the whole thing fell in. That should have never happened. Those bastards in management need to buy heavier cranes, because it was the weight of the lid that dragged him in. That kind of accident can happen in Lackawanna or Buffalo. Thirty fucking six thousand in four fucking plants. And these bastards are going to sit back and tell us we got too many men working in the plants.

"The motherfuckers are too cheap to update the equipment. Too cheap. They're making money on our broken backs, and the only reason they say we're featherbedding is that they want to make even more by having less of us in the plants. They're trying to bust the unions. If we give in, if we fall apart, we can bend over right here tonight and kiss our asses goodbye."

Another roar rose in the hall, a roll of thunder. The men did not believe the charges of featherbedding, but they were worried about what would happen if their numbers were cut. They were the ones who had to face the one truth in the plant: heat.

Each man had had to judge for himself if he could stand it. The closer he worked to the heat, the more money he made. He could work at one of the one-hundred-foot-tall blast furnaces where iron ore, coke, and limestone were smelted. The material, the charge, was fired by stoves bigger than the furnace. Before the iron was tapped from the furnace, it reached temperatures of over 3,000 degrees. The furnaces ran continuously, sometimes for as long as two years. They were down only when their asbestos firebrick linings had to be replaced. If a man had the nerve, he could reline the furnace — don a green asbestos suit, put in his earplugs, pull on his gloves, climb into the furnace only ten hours after it had been shut down, and with a jackhammer begin chipping away at the slag, chipping into the red, then into the white glowing iron and slag. A man who did this worked with a partner, each working for five minutes, then climbing out while the other went down. They were watched by a safety man, who would be responsible for pulling them out if they were burned, if they were injured by the jackhammer, if they looked as if they were going to pass out. After the chipping was done, any damaged bricks were replaced.

If a man could stand more heat, he could work at the open hearth where the steel was made. He could operate the overhead crane, charge the C-pits where the steel was smelted. At the open hearth he could also be a first or second helper, walk around with an asbestos suit and face shield to protect him. Before the steel could be poured into molds, the first helper had to test it. To do this he put on a silver-colored, zinc-rayonized suit over his asbestos one and went out onto a catwalk over the ladle of molten steel where he took a sample. If he were to fall in, as sometimes men did, he had an assurance from Capital that the steel would not be used. A body in the steel spoiled the whole batch, the men were told. The fact of the matter was, a man falling into a 2,500-degree vat of steel was vaporized. And anyway, none of the men would know if a batch was ever dumped, because before any pouring, the floor had to be cleared. A siren was sounded for the men to vacate the area before the explosive was set off, blowing the tap plug and sending the steel flowing into the molds. Two-hundred-pound men could pass out like girls swooning at the sight of blood. They knew they were in hell.

Even those who could stand up to the heat found the cold hard to bear. In winter the men would emerge from hell only to face below-zero temperatures and a fierce northern wind, the Hawk, swooping across Lake Erie at thirty, fifty miles an hour. If it caught them crossing a patch of ice, it would lift them off of their feet, carry them tumbling through the air, and abruptly drop them back to earth.

Tuberculosis and pneumonia were common. Those who stayed too long got black lung, emphysema, cancer. This was the reality the men at Capital had to face. Featherbedding was only a word.

The representative had spoken the truth. Samuel knew the horror of the conditions, and thought there was no way the union could lose. It was on a mission.

On the sixtieth night of the strike, an Irish worker from the rolling mill went out into the back yard of his Capital Park house, which he had eighteen years of payments left on, and while his twelve children and pregnant wife slept, shot himself in the stomach with a .38.

The next day a meeting was called. "One of our own has fallen," said the same red-faced man who had spoken at the previous meetings. "We are bowed, but we will not be defeated."

A collection was taken up for the man's family, and Samuel threw in fifty cents he could not afford to give. He felt defeated. He felt as if someone had fallen upon him and beaten him with a stick. He had had enough of mummering men crammed into rooms. He had grown tired of harangues.

There was to be no miracle, no manna from heaven. Their strike had put one hundred thousand men in other industries out of work, and daily that number grew. Coal miners, auto workers, construction workers, truckers.

As Samuel looked around the room, he felt alone. He recognized a black man he knew from his boarding house, Moses.

Moses was working for a plant manager who walked out with the strikers, "doing this and that," he had told Samuel on day forty-five. "You can get a job too, if you need money."

"Where this man get money?"

"I don't know and I don't care. He got money, but if you can't use a little extra, don't come."

"Who don't need money?" Samuel said. "How long can this strike last?"

"I don't know," Moses said. "Ain't no end in sight. Talk done broke off."

Samuel went along with Moses. Moses was going to the manager's house, Samuel to a company doctor's house. As they walked over the bridge to Capital Heights, Moses asked, "Don't you got a lunch?"

"Naw," Samuel said. "I can make it without lunch."

"Don't you even got some water?"

"Naw, I didn't think to bring none. Don't they got water where we going?"

Samuel's job was to mow and rake the doctor's lawn and split a half cord of wood. It felt good to be working, but he was working on an empty stomach, and by noon, every time his heart beat he felt a rush of blood in his ears. He went to the back door to ask for a drink.

The doctor's wife answered, smiling through the screen door.

"Ma'am, could I get some water, please?" he asked, his eyes cast down.

"Sure," she said, her mouth filled with sugar. "Where's your thermos?"

"Ma'am?"

"Your water bottle? Don't you have one?"

"I forgot it. If it's not too much trouble, ma'am, could I get a glass?"

The smile disappeared from the woman's lips, but her voice was still sweet. "Certainly. You wait right here," she said, and vanished behind the silvery mesh. She returned and carefully opened the door just enough to give him the water. It was in a mayonnaise jar. He quickly drank, left the jar on the steps, and then backed off of the porch.

At the end of the day he was in his room frying a pan of potatoes when Moses came to see him. "How it go?" Moses asked.

Samuel rolled his eyes at him. "I ain't know it was such a short walk to Mississippi."

"It ain't that bad."

Samuel tended his pan. "That woman ain't even want to give me no water. When I saw that, I asked her for a glass. I was testing her."

"Testing her? You must be crazy. Who you think you is, some kind of a goddamn teacher? These white people the ones got the lessons to teach. They the ones do the testing. All you got to do is smile, play things they way, and make the money. The man I work for like me. He be taking me out to his cabin to do work. It's nice out there. You can fish, got a little lake ain't poisoned like Lake Erie."

"All you got to do is be a Uncle Tom."

"You think I'm a Uncle Tom?" Moses asked, raising his voice.

"Let me tell you something. I was a man when I left the South, and I ain't come all this way to be a white-man boy. I'll go back 'fore I do that."

"You talking out your hat now," Moses said. "You know things worser down there. Colored people got a place."

"What, we ain't got a place here?"

"It's a bigger place."

"That don't make it better," Samuel said.

"Yeah it do. You go on back south, then. I'm staying right here, and I'm a tell *you* something. I live better here than there."

"I rather starve than go work on the other side of the bridge," Samuel said, scooping his dinner out of the pan.

"You will," Moses said. "If this strike keep going the way it is, you will."

Despite what Samuel had said to Moses, before he would return to the South, he would disappear. He would keep heading north. Head up to Canada, follow the drinking gourd until it tipped in the sky, raining down its promise, freedom.

But on day sixty-five, relief came. Pickup trucks from local farms rolled up in front of the union hall looking for men to work. They came at six A.M., and Samuel was there, his lunch box packed, his thermos filled with water.

When the strikers were ordered back to work under Taft-Hartley, they did not go. A challenge was mounted. But while the union was fighting the back-to-work order, an agreement was reached between the union and management. Vice President Nixon had helped bring the two sides together. Management had not proven its charges of featherbedding.

Under the agreement no jobs were to be lost. A thirty-nine-cent-per-hour wage-and-benefit package was offered, and it was passed unanimously by the rank and file.

The union's national leader came to a rally in Buffalo to help the men celebrate their victory. Samuel went, not because he felt much like celebrating, but because he wanted to see the man who had so much power, a man who had made Eisenhower back down, a man who held the future of a million men in his mouth.

Samuel was disappointed. The union leader looked like

such an ordinary man, an older white man with silver hair and a two-hundred-dollar double-breasted wool suit. He did not look as if he had ever been inside a steel plant, and he did not look tired. It had been one hundred sixteen days, and he did not look as if he had gone hungry.

The men barely let him enter the hall. They surrounded him, hoisted him on their shoulders, and carried him up to the podium. While a band played "Happy Days Are Here Again," the leader yelled out through a crackling microphone, "Victory is yours!"

That had been four years ago.

A man can spin silences around himself like eggshells, each silence an opaque, perfect, elliptical world. Enclosed in his own white silence, Samuel sat in the middle of the living room floor among the Easter eggs, his knees drawn to his chest. Over an hour had passed since Mary Kate had gone up to bed. It was cold in the living room, and he got up from the floor. Though he tried to step carefully through the mine field of eggs, he stepped on one and crushed it as he weaved his way.

The bedroom was dark. Samuel began undressing. He started when Mary Kate's voice came to him.

"I ain't mean what I say," she said.

Samuel was still undressing. He turned toward her voice, a small and warm flame.

"You right," he said. "I was sitting downstairs thinking. I'm a get up with you in the morning and make a fool out myself."

"You ain't got to get up," she said.

"I know I don't *got* to."

"Your mind done been busy. There been that hearsay of a strike."

Samuel stood only a few feet away from her, completely naked.

"You don't think I heard it?"

Samuel was silent.

"Where you at?" she asked.

"I'm here." He walked over to the bed and lay down behind her on his side. "I ain't know you heard 'bout it," he said, moving close to her.

"I can read. It's been in the paper, and you know how colored folks talk, anyway. Hear say folks went hungry last time."

Mary Kate turned toward him. She could feel Samuel's chest rise and fall. "It's true. Folks went hungry. It was hard times," he said. "I ain't want to worry you with no talk like that."

"Seeing you starve yourself was what was worrying me, and lying, saying you was eating someplace else. Wasn't nothing for me to say. It was for you to say."

The muscles in Samuel's back were tense. They began twitching, and then there was a soft fluttering, like bird wings. Mary Kate rubbed his back, calming the muscles, trying to free what was trapped inside.

"I was scared," he whispered, his head resting on her shoulder. His tears soaked into her cotton gown. Her fingers flowed over his back. He was pulled into sleep, and when he awoke the next morning to hear his son calling out from his room, he arose in the blue morning light, still a man.

5

FIRE

HENRY'S MOTHER came home from work to find him with his head in the oven and his friend Skip sitting on the kitchen sink.

When Skip saw her coming through the living room, he tried to save himself. He jumped from the sink and dashed out the back door. As he jumped off the porch and into the yard, he let out a yell. "This yard full of shit!"

Two men in hip boots were standing nearby. "All the yards are," one said. "The sewers are backed up. Get out of the yard, boy. We're trying to work."

"You get in here, Skipper," Henry's mother yelled. "Get your butt in here right now."

"Yes, ma'am," Skip said, and sloshed back through the ankle-deep water.

"And you, Henry. Get your head out that oven."

But Henry did not move. "Just one more minute," he said. Then he began to scream. His mother grabbed him by the shoulders and pulled him out.

"You look like a fool," she said. "You satisfied now you look like Skipper?"

Skip had just stepped inside the back door. "It look tough, Henry. I think it took."

"Hold it right there, boy. Take off them shitty pants and shoes in my house," Henry's mother said.

"But ma'am."

"Don't you 'but ma'am' me. You do what I say, boy. You the one talked Henry into this, with your slick head."

Skip stepped back onto the porch and stripped down to his underwear. The men whistled and laughed, and Skip jumped back inside the house.

"It's really burning now, man. You think you should wash it out?" Henry asked.

"You go get Skipper some pants. He almost a damn grown man, standing here in his drawers."

"Yes, ma'am," Henry said, and flew upstairs. His head was on fire. If Skip did not wash the lye from his head soon, he would start screaming again.

"Burning part of it," Skip had told him as he raked a comb full of white, lye-based cream through Henry's hair. "The first time I had my process, shoot, man, I was howling like a dog. But it took real good. Like with you, when I finish with you, I'm a put your head in the oven for a couple minutes. That's going to send it, man. That's going to cook it. All the tough conks you see was finished off in the oven."

To grow his hair long enough for the process, Henry had to get out of going to the barbershop every Saturday for two months. It had been easy during the summer. He had been working a summer job at the plant. But once school started, his mother wanted his hair cut. She had taken his two younger brothers, and they had come back with their heads shaved. Henry had had to keep coming up with excuses.

"Next week, Mama."

"I have to get my pants out layaway today."

"They having football tryouts today."

"I hurt my knee at tryouts last Saturday. I can't walk to Ridge Road."

Every day Skip would pull Henry's hair up from his scalp. "It's getting there, man. It's getting there."

"Yeah, man. It's going to have to get there soon. My mama fenna take a razor to my head any day now," Henry had said.

This was the day it had gotten there. It would be Saturday tomorrow, and Henry didn't know if he could bluff his way out of the barber's chair again. He and Skip went right home after school. Henry ran upstairs and got a towel, a comb, and the jar of cream he had hidden in his dresser drawer.

When Skip first applied the cream to Henry's scalp, it felt cool. Henry could feel it working. He could feel the naps sliding out of his hair. The comb was gliding through, flying through his slick hair.

Then the fire started. Just a flicker at the base of his neck. And then, as if fanned by some unseen wind, it spread all over his scalp.

"It's burning, man," Henry said.

Skip stood over him, still raking the hard plastic comb over his scalp. "I'm fenna put you in the oven now," Skip said.

And two minutes after Skip stuck Henry's head in the oven, Henry's mother walked in.

"Here the pants," Henry said. "Rinse me now, Skip."

Skip slipped on the pants and went to the sink to put out the fire on Henry's scalp. He turned on the water, and a few drops fell on top of Henry's head. They could hear the singing of air in the pipes.

"Ain't no water, man. They cut the water off," Skip said.

Henry began screaming again, and his mother opened the back door. "What happened to the water?" she asked the men in the yard.

"It's off, ma'am. We cut it off at noon to unclog the sewer. It'll be back on by five," one of the men said.

But it was barely four, and Henry could not wait until five. "Go put your head in the toilet," his mother said. "Hurry now, before that stuff burn you."

Henry and Skip ran upstairs to the bathroom, and Henry dunked his head into the bowl of the tankless toilet.

Skip grabbed the soap dish and tried to dip some of the water from the bowl over Henry's head. But it did little good.

"I'm a kill you, man," Henry said.

"How was I supposed to know they turned the water off?"

Henry's mother entered the bathroom with a six-pack of Pepsi and began pouring the pops over her son's head. "Go next door on either side of me and see if anyone saved some water," she told Skip.

Skip took off and left Henry alone with his mother. The Pepsi was putting out the fire and tingling his scalp. His mother was gently wiping the lye from his head.

Skip returned with a pot and a pitcher of water, and Henry's mother finished rinsing his head in the sink. She managed to get all of the lye out.

"You going to let me keep it? Can I keep it, Mama? I'm almost a man, Mama. I'm a senior. Can't I wear my hair like I want?" Henry pleaded.

"It's your head," his mother said, and walked out of the bathroom.

Henry stood there with tears in his eyes, and Skip ran his fingers through Henry's hair. "It's tough," Skip said. "It's really tough."

6

GROUNDED

"PETER PAN a faggot. He a boy they say can fly, but I don't think no boy can fly. That's stupid. Rick, this boy that moved 'round my block, me and him climbed our row roof and jumped off. It was snow on the ground. It looked like a lot of snow. It wasn't. I didn't want to jump first. I pushed Rick. He screamed all the way down. The snow didn't break his fall. He broke his leg. They couldn't get me off. They had to call the fire trucks, and then I ran from the men when they was on the roof. It was dark then. That's why I think Peter Pan stupid. Can't no boy fly. I don't want to fly nohow. I want to drive me a Cadillac."

Isaac sat down after he read his report. "That's interesting," the teacher said. "You seem to be saying you don't like the book because you find it unbelievable, and Peter somewhat . . . childlike. But that was the whole point of the book."

"Naw, I'm saying he a faggot."

"Don't use that word," the teacher said.

"Why? You asked me to write what I feel about the book. Now you telling me I'm wrong," Isaac said.

"That's not what I'm saying at all. Let's move on to the next report," the teacher said.

"Fuck you," Isaac said under his breath. He didn't know why he was thrown into this school with these people. They were stupid, retards, jellyheads.

It was after he mowed down half the fence at Roosevelt Junior High that he was transferred. It wasn't even his fault. The men had been tearing up a field to expand the parking lot. Isaac and Rick had gone there one night to see if they could get a piece of the equipment to work. They couldn't get the tractor or the bulldozer to start, but Rick managed to get the steamroller started. Isaac was the one who set it in motion. He was playing with the levers, and the steamroller began moving forward. It took off in a slow and steady line, crunching over gravel. Isaac was excited. He felt powerful atop the machine. It was moving like a tank.

"We at war, Ricky. We killing the Japs."

"You crazy, Isaac. I'm not playing no stupid war game with you."

"We killing 'em. We at war with them Commie bastards. We going to show 'em not to be messing with us," Isaac said.

Rick was the one who saw the fence. It seemed to pop up in front of them right out of the night. He screamed for Isaac to stop.

"I can't stop it," Isaac yelled.

Rick jumped off the side and rolled across the gravel. Isaac was too scared to jump. He could see himself tripping and getting his bones crushed to dust under the runaway machine.

"I'm riding it out, Rick. I'm going through this mind field.

If I don't make it out alive, give my Purple Heart to my mama."

"You crazy, Isaac. You really crazy. Bail out, man. Bail out!"

Isaac stayed on, and they heard sirens. Rick took off, turned himself into a shadow and vanished in the darkness, but Isaac was caught. He was placed in the custody of his father. No charges were pressed against him, but the next morning he had to bring his parents to school.

"You go see 'bout that hard-head boy," his mother said to his father. "I'm too shame to go, and say what to them white people — the fool didn't mean to run down the fence? Far as I know, he did it on purpose."

So his father went. Before his hands had even opened, he was sitting before the principal with his hat on his knees and his head bowed. The fence had to be paid for.

Isaac sat quietly until the principal said, "It would be best to place your son in occupational education."

"O.E.? No!" Isaac said. "I'm not going to a school for retards. I'm not riding the blue cheese."

"Isaac, you be quiet when the man is talking," his father reprimanded.

"I'm not going to no school for jellyheads."

"Isaac, set there and be good," his father said.

That was when the principal told Isaac he would have to leave the office. Isaac stood outside the door feeling as if he were going to throw up. He knew his record. He had failed the seventh grade once, and he was on his way to a second trip through the eighth grade.

That wasn't his fault either. He was bored. They were always trying to teach him things he did not want to know, and there were always tricks. He had to find themes in stories, and write thesis statements, and make paragraphs.

In seventh grade there had been sentence diagramming. That wrecked two whole years for him. Seeing a sentence all strung out, dangling from a line with parts of it sticking off of it like branches from a tree, made Isaac want to crawl out on one of those branches and hang himself from a particle, or article, or something. His teacher would put a sentence on the board like

> When the black cat crept around the corner of the white fence, the brown and tan spotted dog gave chase.

and Isaac would say, "That dog stupid to be chasing a black cat. Don't he know black cats bad luck?" Then he would be asked to be quiet, to just do his work or leave the room.

And he was always being asked to draw three-dimensional pictures of boxes and rectangles, and to measure lines, and to find the area of a square.

> If a man has 77 cords of wood, and his neighbor borrows 10 and burns them, only to discover he had 32 cords of wood in his own barn, how many cords would the man and his neighbor each have if the neighbor returned the wood he borrowed?

Isaac could not bear it. There were too many numbers and words thrown together. He would start wondering what a cord was, and why the neighbor borrowed wood if he already had wood, and why couldn't the neighbor borrow more wood than the man had? That was a real test for negative numbers. And why didn't the neighbor just chop down a tree in the first place, and how could the neighbor return wood that he burned, anyway?

He was thrown out of school for three days because of negative numbers.

Isaac knew very well there were negative numbers, but he wasn't interested in them. The teacher told him to think of them as money.

"They not money. If we going to talk about money, let's talk about money."

"Well, O.K.," the teacher said. She handed Isaac ten pennies, and Isaac put them in his pants pocket.

"Now let me have them back," the teacher said, and she put out her hand.

"Naw, man. You a Indian giver. They mines."

"Isaac, stop this. Work with me on this one. Give me the pennies."

Isaac dug into his pocket and retrieved the change.

"See, now I'm in debt for ten pennies. I started with zero. Now I'm minus ten."

"That ain't right. Them your ten pennies, and you took 'em back. Indian giver," Isaac said.

"Maybe this will help," the teacher said. She put the money in his pocket. "Let's pretend for a minute. Work with me now. Let's say you owned the pennies —"

"Then I was robbed," Isaac said. "Talking 'bout give you the money. That's robbery where I come from."

"Isaac, be serious. You have to let me help you."

Isaac sighed. "All right."

"Now, you owned the money, and then *loaned* them to me, and I spent them. Since I started with zero, I would owe you ten less than I have. Let's say then that my husband gave me twenty pennies, and I paid you back, how many would I have?" the teacher asked.

"Ten," Isaac said.

"Very good!" the teacher bellowed.

But Isaac would have none of it. In a fit, he tore down the number line over the chalkboard and ripped it up. "Isaac crazy," the students screamed, and then he got three days' suspension.

But as long as Isaac was quiet, his teachers didn't bother him. He asked to be excused almost every period to go to the bathroom, or get a drink, or blow his nose. He roamed the halls.

Down in the bowels of the school Isaac saw enormous furnaces that roared like dragons. In another part of the basement he found cots and cans of food, gigantic silver cans covered with dust. They were big enough to be eaten by monsters, he thought. Why, a monster could eat the cans whole.

Once a year the whole school went to visit the cots and cans. Isaac loved the air-raid drill. In case of a war, everyone would stay down there and eat the canned food and sleep on the cots. But there were only about fifty cots, and three hundred people could fit in the shelter. A yellow and black sign at the entrance to the shelter told you that. Isaac knew there were more than five hundred students in the school, plus teachers. Now *that* was a test for negative numbers. But he figured he wouldn't be one of those minuses. He wouldn't be less than zero. He would be the first one down there, slide right down the wooden banisters all the way from the third floor, and then sprint down the basement stairs. He would eat canned beef and powdered eggs until all the Commies were dead.

When Isaac was in the seventh grade for the second time, a white boy in the eighth grade, a boy no bigger than a ten-year-old, was caught stealing a can of food and was suspended for three days. He was one of fifteen children, and his family lived in a run-down house near the school. "Stupid Polack," Isaac had said. "Greedy gut. What he want? For us to go hungry in a atomic war?"

Isaac had explored much of the universe by wandering the halls of the school. There were rats in cages, dead newts in jars, sewing machines, maps of other countries and globes that would bounce like balls, charts of the human body full of veins or muscles or bones, strange boxes in the girls' lavatories that read "Modess." Isaac knew where the janitors ate lunch and when the oil delivery truck came. He knew if you turned the gas on high in the lab and then threw a lit match at it, you could blast your eyebrows and lashes right off of your face. He also knew that if you closed yourself inside a locker, you couldn't let yourself out, and that the fat dictionary in the library had nasty words in it. Isaac knew lots of things, all kinds of things. But still he was failing. That was what the principal was telling his father, that he was stupid, a loser.

Isaac was transferred the next week to the Occupational Education Center in Capital Park, despite his protestations. A tour impressed him, though he would not admit it. There were all kinds of shops, a machine shop, a woodworking shop, even an auto shop. He was told that he would spend half the day in shop and half in classes.

Isaac didn't mind the school that much. It was better than Roosevelt, really. During his first month there he hadn't been asked to diagram a sentence, to add or subtract negative numbers, to draw one geometric shape. In wood shop he learned how to drive a nail and turn a screw. He was even taught how to use a saw, not just the handsaw but the power saw too. He made his own tool box and a pencil box, and he had been allowed to burn his name into the side of each. Now he was working on a footstool for his father.

Isaac's English teacher was beginning to spoil things, though, with this Peter Pan thing. What did he want Isaac to say? He wrote what he felt, and now he felt wrong. Why couldn't you call Peter Pan a faggot? All Isaac knew was that if some boy with those fairy boots came through *his* window, talking about his shadow wouldn't stick to him, he would have beat him up. He would have pushed Pete right back out the window, just like he pushed Rick from the roof, and then he would watch him hit the ground. *Foop!* Pete would grow up then, some stupid white boy with fairy boots and a broken leg, and a shadow all balled up on the ground.

If he had been back at Roosevelt, this would have been the time to roam. During his first few weeks at the new school, Isaac had wandered down to the basement. He had heard sounds coming from one of the rooms there. What he heard sounded like animals, but when he peeked inside, he saw a room full of jellyheads.

They were sitting around some tables with teachers. Their bodies were soft and doll-like. Some were twisted and bent into unnatural positions, some strapped in wheelchairs, some wearing helmets.

One boy knelt in a corner, a helmet strapped to his head, and he was banging, banging, banging his head on the cement floor.

Isaac was staring at this boy when one of the children at a table pointed at him and began making noises. "Ooh ah coa ah coa ah," Isaac heard him say.

A teacher turned to Isaac and smiled. "He's asking you to come in. Would you like to come join us?"

Isaac took off running, tripping as he climbed the stairs. He got up and kept running, not looking behind him, and he hadn't gone back to the basement since.

If a boy could really fly, these were the children he should take, Isaac thought. He should take these retards and dump them in Never Land.

7

NOVEMBER 22, 1963

JUST WHEN there were no more tears, he died. As she lay on the couch with the television playing to no one, he died again. Just when her eyes were closing and her tears were grains of salt in the corners of her eyes, she blinked, and in a splash of whiteness he died.

A pebble thrown into the ocean at noon, cold and white and hard, splashing water on her. Salty water drying, leaving white rings of salt around her swollen ankles.

"Mrs. Taylor, you should not eat salt while you're expecting. It causes swelling."

But she was not a salt eater. It was starch she ate, boxes and boxes of Argo. What a country thing to do. She fed it to Mikey and kissed the whiteness from his lips before his father came home.

And she was no dirt eater, like some women in All-Bright Court, sending down south for boxes of earth to eat. She did not eat it when she was back home, even when the women sucked on it to cut their hunger and fed it to children like candy. She never ate it, though they said it was sweet. She ate starch because she was pregnant, sometimes a box a week, and it left her dry.

She had found out she was pregnant a few weeks before Easter when her mouth was searching for starch. It led her and Mikey across the field at the end of All-Bright Court and to the Red Store, a store the people named for its color, the redness of the bricks. Never did they call it Jablonski's Market. It was there in the Red Store that an old man was telling a story to the man behind the counter, a story of a snake.

The old man's cousin had been bitten by a cottonmouth. He was bitten on the shank, and he ignored it. But he had gotten sick some days later, boils rose on him, and a fever burned in his chest. Then the boils erupted, and cotton burst forth from them, cotton white and light as air. Black people ran from him, but some white men came from the state college, thinking he was going to die, thinking maybe they could figure out a way to farm cotton out of a nigger. They collected the cotton and measured it. But when the fever broke, the cotton dried up. The white men went away disappointed. The black people came around again. They didn't know if he had really been bitten by a cottonmouth. He could have ended up that way from picking cotton all those years. Maybe it had gotten into his blood.

Mrs. Taylor did not believe the old man's story. It seemed every week someone was coming up from down south with all kinds of country tales. But the thought of the snake and the cotton sickened her, and she threw up right there in the store. She wanted to clean up after herself, but she didn't have a tissue. Mr. Jablonski had to clean up.

The storytelling man looked at her and her son. He looked at the box of starch in her hand. "What you want this time, a girl?"

She did not say anything to the man. She paid for the

starch and left. But this storytelling man knew, knew before even she had suspected. Mary Kate understood that the snake story wasn't true, but that did not stop it from upsetting her. That did not stop it from slithering, wet and cold, back to her.

It came back to her on this day, many months later, after her tears were salt. He was shot again, splash. The snake encircled her ankles. The cottonmouth crawled up her shanks. She could not see it, she was drowning in darkness, but she could feel its heaviness on her legs, pulling her down, back into darkness. And then there was the bite, wet and sharp. She awakened, screaming and beating her legs.

Mikey was lying across her lap, biting her.

"Boy, what you was doing there? Why was you biting Mama?"

"What happened to your stories, Mama? They not on."

The phone rang. She did not answer it. He would be dying there, on the line, in someone's mouth.

"That why you was biting me?" she asked.

"Can I go play in the snow?"

"I'll see," she said.

"I didn't have no lunch, Mama . . . The phone ringing."

"I know," she said, and got up from the couch. She turned off the television. He was dying in there, in some white man's mouth. "Mama fenna make you some lunch. Come on."

"You was crying, Mama . . . The phone ringing," Mikey said.

"I know," she said.

He was dying there, and she wiped the salt away. How many times could one man die?

8

THUNDERBIRD

"So we got a new President," the butcher at the A & P said to Moses as he wrapped up the smoked turkey Venita had ordered for Thanksgiving.

"Johnson ain't new. He been in there a year. People voted for him 'cause of JFK. That's why I voted for him."

"Get out," the butcher said. "You're in the U.S.W. If they thought you voted for Goldwater, they would bounce you. No, first they would collect your dues. Then they would give you the bum's rush. Hey, what happened to your hand? You get burned or something?"

"Naw," Moses said. "When that wind was kicking up last week, I slipped on some ice coming out the Welfare Building and broke my wrist."

"Well, I hope Capital is taking care of you. That company is a damn money tree," the butcher said. "I used to work for them, you know."

"Is that right?" Moses said.

"Yeah, but there wasn't enough money being shaken my

way. I hear things are better now. You get that thirteen-week vacation."

"Right," Moses said sarcastically. "Ten years from now I should get it."

The U.S.W. president had negotiated a thirteen-week sabbatical once every five years for workers in the top half of the seniority rank of their plants. Though Moses scoffed at the paid vacation because his would be so far in the future, the sabbatical was a major victory for the workers. An average member of the rank and file would be able to take three or four before he retired.

"Word is, the union president got us this deal so he can look good. There's a election coming up. But I ain't voting for him. He the one led that strike back in 'fifty-nine. We ain't had a raise since then. But he making fifty thousand," Moses said. "I don't see how he expect us to live. I ain't hardly making it." He pulled out money to pay for the turkey.

"You pay for it at the front check-out."

Despite what Moses told the butcher, he was doing very well. He was making $4.00 an hour when the average steelworker's wage was $3.70. He was still paying on the three rooms of furniture he and Venita had bought, but he managed to put money away. He had even gotten a car, a brand-new 1964 Thunderbird, a beautiful red hardtop with bucket seats. Moses had ordered the optional lights that told him when the fuel was low and a door was ajar.

Venita thought those features were a waste of money. "How you wouldn't know you didn't have gas? And there ain't but two doors on the car. It seem like you would know if one of them was open," she said to Moses.

This car was for their trip down south. There was no way

Moses wanted to arrive in Starkville on a bus. He was going back in style, in a car that moved people "in a special atmosphere."

But he and Venita never made the trip. When Goodman, Chaney, and Schwerner were unearthed in Philadelphia, Mississippi, Venita refused to go. "I don't want to be on the road," she told Moses, "not down there. I can see my people some other time."

"We ain't going that far south, and we ain't going down there to start no trouble," Moses said.

"You believe they was starting trouble? Them crackers killed them for the fun of it. Don't be stupid."

He hid within the shell of his words. They were a way of protecting him from the truth. He did not believe the three men were agitators. They were close to his age. One of them was black, Chaney. Moses knew what could happen to a black man on a lonely road in Mississippi. Goodman and Schwerner learned what could happen even to white men.

Moses and Venita took a proletariat vacation to Atlantic City instead.

On his way to pay for his turkey, Moses passed down the dairy aisle. A small boy dressed in a snowsuit was leaning over the case. The boy opened a carton and began dropping eggs, one by one, to the floor. Moses was about to say something to the boy when he saw Samuel Taylor coming up the aisle pulling a red wagon filled with groceries.

"Mikey, what is you doing?" Samuel yelled as Mikey was dropping another egg.

Moses rushed past the pair without looking at them. He paid for his turkey and left the store. His car was parked in the gravel lot in back. As Moses neared his car, he saw a woman and a gaggle of children coming up the street. It was Greene and her brood.

That summer Greene and her six children had come up from Florida. They just showed up at All-Bright Court in a dusty yellow pickup that broke down the day they arrived and had to be towed away. No one knew them, and not a week after they moved in, the bats came.

Out of the twilight they appeared as shadows, first a few, then hundreds. But under the pale light of the full moon they became bats. Isaac led a group of boys on a bat hunt. With brooms and sticks they managed to kill a few bats they chased off from the main group. No one had ever seen anything like it before, and when one of the women mentioned it to Greene, she said, "I want to get my hands on one of them bats. I could use one of them bats."

And that was all it had taken. The next morning, the question "What she want with a bat?" was being asked by the women from one end of All-Bright Court to the other.

"Where them bats come from out of nowhere and then just disappear?"

"You reckon she called them?"

"And *what* she was doing with a bat?"

"What you think! She into hoodoo."

"Mark my words, she going to hoodoo somebody."

"Hey, girl, you see her teeth? Looking into her mouth make you feel like falling in a pit."

All of Greene's teeth were covered in gold, and none of the women knew how she could afford them. Despite the fact she wore a wedding band, no husband came north with her. And Greene had no trouble attracting men.

"Country nigger" is what the women said of Greene. Of the men they said, "Only a country nigger would think her mouth look good."

Greene was accused of not leaving her country ways behind. Her accusers knew, because they were country niggers
too. Over the years they had claimed to be from Birmingham, Fayetteville, Jacksonville, Jackson, New Orleans. But
they were really from Plain Dealing, Zenith, Goshen, Acme,
Gopher. They had come from specks on the map. They
knew the country and its ways well. They had seen spells
cast, fields dry up, floods come, moles cast in women's
wombs. And then there were the bats.

The bats had come with Greene's arrival. This did not
stop some of the husbands in All-Bright Court from passing
in and out of her back door. They came to explore the riches
of her mouth. They left knowing the secrets beneath her
tongue.

All of her children wore asafetida bags around their
necks. The bags and strings turned black and greasy and
smelled of garlic.

In the parking lot Moses rolled down the car window
with his good hand and spoke to Greene as she passed with
her children. "Cold enough for you?"

"I'm telling you, I done moved to the coldest place there
is," Greene said.

"It ain't all of that. You get used to it. Your blood get
thicker," Moses said. Even in the thin air, he thought he
could smell the rankness of the bags. He did not believe in
their power, or hers. His wife, Venita, thought Greene to
be a conjure woman, a woman whose power should not be
overlooked.

"You must have a hole in your head if you thinking 'bout
going to her. How many times I got to tell you you ain't in
the country no more," Moses had told Venita.

Samuel came around the corner, pulling the Radio Flyer
stuffed with so many bags of groceries that Mikey, who was

sitting in the wagon, had to hold a bag on his lap. Samuel walked with his head bowed to the wind, the wagon skidding on the newly fallen snow.

As they approached the lot, Moses cranked up the window. Silently, he watched Samuel and the boy pass his car and continue down the sidewalk. Then he gunned the engine of his sleek red Thunderbird and flew right by them.

9

SHARERS

SOMEWHERE in the field, hidden among the tall weeds, was a hungry boy. He was lying on his stomach, stuffing slices of bologna in his mouth. He put so many pieces in his mouth that he gagged, and a ball of pink flesh fell out into the weeds.

"Kiss it up to God," he said, and kissed the meat. He began eating it, pulling off a few twigs and an ant as he ate.

"Dennis," a voice called from somewhere in the field. "Where you at, Dennis? My mama want to talk to you."

The boy stopped eating. He pitched the half-eaten meat over his shoulder and lay still. He would not come out of hiding because the pack of bologna he was lying on, he had stolen from the Red Store.

He had put the cold package inside his pants, but before he could get to the door, Mr. Jablonski was shouting, "Hey you, hey boy," coming from behind the counter with a bat in his hand. Dennis beat him to the door just as Mrs. Taylor, Mikey, and the baby, Dorene, were coming in. He knocked Dorene to the ground and escaped.

"Don't ever come back in my store! If I see you again, I'll beat your brains out," Mr. Jablonski screamed.

Mrs. Taylor bent to pick up Dorene.

"No, I'll get her," Mr. Jablonski said as he picked up the crying child. "You're in no shape to be bending like that."

"Don't his mama got credit with you?" Mrs. Taylor asked.

"I cut her off. She never pays me. Every time she gets her check she has a story, or she doesn't show up at all. I'm in business here, you know."

"The boy hungry. It's a shame."

"It's a shame, but what can you do?" Mr. Jablonski said as he returned behind the counter.

At one time Mary Kate thought there was something she could do. The boy had begun showing up on her doorstep not long after Mikey started kindergarten. Before she ever saw him, Mikey had come home with stories of Dennis.

"He never be having milk money. He always be a sharer, Mama."

"What's a sharer?"

"When you don't bring in milk money, Mrs. Franco split a milk and let you have some."

"That's nice of her," Mikey's mother said.

"Yeah, Mama, but the kids that be sharing all the time be nasty. This boy Dennis, he colored, and he stink. This little white girl be so dirty. Them two always be sharing. Kids be picking on them."

"I hope you not one of them, Mikey. They can't help the way they is."

Mikey was silent. Once he had stuck out his tongue at them when Mrs. Franco wasn't looking. The other children laughed. It was fun. But one Monday toward the end of October, the fun stopped.

Mikey left home with five pennies knotted in a handkerchief, but when he arrived at school, they were gone. He had to share a milk that day with Dennis.

The little white girl shared one with a Puerto Rican girl. All four of them sat at a small table and had their milk in Dixie cups. Mikey did not want to drink his. He didn't even want the windmill cookies Mrs. Franco passed out. He sat staring at the three others at his table.

The white girl drank all her chocolate milk with one lifting of her cup, and there was a brown mustache on her face. Mikey stared at her whiteness. Tiny green veins pulsed around her gray eyes. Thin streams of dirt ran down her arms. She didn't say anything to Mikey, but when she saw him staring, she opened her mouth full of cookies. Mikey turned from her and looked at the Puerto Rican girl.

She looked clean. Her black hair was swept up in a single ponytail and curled in a tight corkscrew. There were gold hoops in her ears. She never looked up from the table, though. She ate slowly, taking careful bites and cautious sips.

Mikey glanced to his side, at Dennis. He had already finished and was licking the crumbs from his napkin.

"Dennis, stop that," Mrs. Franco said.

Dennis smiled. "Them some good cookies, Mike. Don't you like 'em?"

"I had milk money," Mikey said.

"Don't you like them cookies?" Dennis asked.

Mikey stared at the boy's hair. It was uncombed and matted. "You eat 'em."

Dennis grabbed the cookies and stuffed both of them into his mouth, hardly bothering to chew them.

"I'm glad you here, 'cause they don't talk. That one stupid," Dennis said, pointing at the white girl. "The other one stupid too. She can't even speak no English. You hear her in class? 'Monita conita Frito corn chips.'"

Mikey wanted to laugh, but he remembered why he was at the table with the sharers. "I ain't supposed to be here. I lost my money. I ain't going sit here tomorrow."

"Oh," Dennis said. "You want your milk?"

Mikey did not sit with the sharers the next day. His mother had money to send, four pennies knotted in a handkerchief, pinned in his pocket. He had his own milk, in a carton, the way milk was supposed to be. He had a straw and blew bubbles. Sharers never got straws. He did not want to look over to where they sat, but he did, and each time he looked over, Dennis smiled or waved. "Mike," he silently mouthed. Mikey smiled.

Mikey had found a friend. Dennis began following him home from school. He and Mikey would play until it was time for dinner.

"You got to go home now," Mikey's mother or father would say.

The boy would leave Mikey's house, but he wouldn't go home. He would play by himself out back or disappear around the end of the row, only to return in ten or fifteen minutes, asking, "Can Mike come out?"

One Friday night in late November, Mr. Taylor went out to empty the trash and found Dennis squatting next to the back step.

"Boy, you crazy? What you doing out in the snow?"

"Can Mike come out?"

"No, Mike can't come out. It's seven o'clock. You better get on home."

"My mama ain't home."

Mr. Taylor put the garbage in the can and stared at the boy. The boy did not head for home. He stood there looking at the ground until Mr. Taylor invited him in and then went up to bed.

Mrs. Taylor fed him a bowl of black-eyed peas and a piece

of corn bread. Dennis ate the bread and peas, and licked the bowl.

"You want some more?" Mrs. Taylor asked.

"Yeah. Them good beans."

"You got a good appetite, Dennis. Mikey won't eat peas. He had peanut butter and jelly for dinner."

Dennis did not say anything. He ate.

At nine Mrs. Taylor woke up her husband. "Sam, take Dennis home."

Mr. Taylor walked Dennis around to 125 to find the front door sitting wide open. There were no lights on in the house.

"My mama not back."

"Well, I'll take you on in and you can turn on the lights and wait for her."

"We don't got no electric. Mama say we going get it back on when she get her check."

Mr. Taylor let out a big blast of white steam through his nose. He did not know what to do, so he brought the boy back home with him.

"You just couldn't leave him there," Mrs. Taylor said. "He just a baby."

"I don't know about all that. I don't want to get in no trouble keeping him here, Mary Kate."

"My mama don't care," Dennis said.

Mr. Taylor let out a blow like he did outside. "I just didn't know what to do. I guess he can stay. I'm tired now, Kate. I'm pulling that double tomorrow. Just put him to bed," Mr. Taylor said, and he went upstairs.

Mrs. Taylor ran a bath for Dennis and told him to get in the tub. When she returned to the bathroom a few minutes later, Dennis was playing in the water, and his pants, shirt, and socks were on the floor. They all smelled of urine.

"Where your underclothes?"

"I don't got none clean."

"Hand me that rag, boy. I'm going to bathe you 'cause you not doing nothing but playing."

"My mama let me wash myself."

"It seem your mama let you do a lot of things," Mrs. Taylor said, and she descended on Dennis with the rough white cloth. "Stand up."

Dennis stood while Mrs. Taylor scrubbed every inch of his body. "You a dirty boy," she said. "Stand right there while I get some alcohol."

She went to the hall closet while Dennis stood shaking in the tub. Where was it Mrs. Taylor thought he would go?

She returned and poured half the bottle over his body and the other half in the tub. She continued to wash the boy and talk to him. "Look at this. Look at this." Dennis looked. It was dirt. He did not know if he was supposed to say something.

After the bath, Mrs. Taylor rubbed Vaseline into his cold, raw skin. She dressed him in a pair of Mikey's pajamas and put him to bed. In the morning she made fried eggs, grits with redeye gravy, and buttered toast with grape jelly. She dressed Dennis, Mikey, and Dorene, and they walked to Dennis's house.

On the way, she rehearsed her speech: What kind of mother is you? Leaving a boy alone. Your child hungry and dirty. You send him out with no drawers on. What if something happen to him? What people going to think? You should . . .

Dennis led them to the front door. It was closed. "My mama home."

She was lying on the couch, sleeping. She opened her eyes. Mrs. Taylor thought she looked like a lizard in a dress. Her eyes were yellow, and the skin on her thin legs was dry and cracked. Her short, reddish hair was standing straight up on her head.

"I'm home, Mama."

"Where you was at?"

"Mike's house. This here his mama," Dennis said, gently pushing Mrs. Taylor closer to the couch.

"Hey," the woman said. "Dennis, go get me some water. You want some water, some water . . . What your name?"

"Mary Kate."

"I'm Cynthia. Want some water?"

"No, I got to be going. I got some wash to do," Mary Kate said, and began backing toward the door, Dorene on her hip. "Let's go, children."

She saved her speech for Samuel. He was so tired that he only half listened.

"You can't save the world, Kate," he said.

Dennis continued to come around. Sometimes he would show up three or four days in a row, and sometimes a week or more would pass without his coming by. The last time he had come, the Taylors were on their way to the circus in Buffalo.

"Go home," Mr. Taylor had told him. "You ain't going to the circus with us."

Mikey's father did not understand. He and Dennis were going to be bareback riders. Mrs. Taylor had taken the boys up to Ridge Road, to the Jubilee, to see *Toby Tyler*. In a few years they would run away and join a circus. They would ride on the backs of horses, and have a clever monkey for a pet. They would wear tights and do tricks and eat candy apples and cotton candy. Toby Tyler would be at the circus tonight, and Dennis would miss it.

Dennis did not move. He stood in the living room staring at the floor. His voice was just a whisper. "My mama say don't be letting ya'll clean me up. I'm clean enough. Ya'll got to take me the way I is."

Mr. Taylor opened the front door to put the boy out, but Mikey ran to him and clung to the boy. He grabbed Dennis around the waist. He held on while his father tried to pull them apart.

"Stop, Mikey. I'm going to whip your ass. Stop."

Mikey and Dennis fell to the floor, and Mrs. Taylor ran downstairs with Dorene in her arms.

"Samuel, what you doing?"

"Ya'll stop," he yelled at the boys. He finally pulled them apart and hurled Dennis out the door. "Don't you come back 'round here, hear me? I don't want you 'round my boy, you goddamn piss pot."

"Sam, he just a boy. He ain't much more than a baby."

"He ain't no baby. Him and Mikey the same age. And you, Michael, I don't want the boy 'round this house. I don't want you talking to a boy like that. He trash. That nasty boy coming here and telling me his whore of a mammy say don't clean him up, we got to take him like he is. So white people be saying, 'See, you smell that? They all stink. They all nasty.' "

"His mama say that? As good as we been to that boy, as many nights he done sat at our table and ate like he lived here?"

"What you expect? The woman a alcoholic. She ain't got sense enough to pay her bills. We done all we can do for that boy. You feed him one day, he hungry the next. You clean him up today, he dirty tomorrow. This thing done gone too far. And you expecting! It's too much, Kate. Too much."

"I'm not going to the stupid circus," Mikey said. "I don't want to go without Dennis."

"Oh yeah, you going, and you going to like it, too. I could've been putting in some overtime today, but I didn't so ya'll could go to the circus. You get on upstairs till your mama call you, 'cause I'm this close to setting a fire to your ass."

Toby Tyler was not at the circus. Mikey did not care. He had a good time without him, and without Dennis. He ate cotton candy and a candy apple. There was a clown who fascinated Mikey.

The clown coughed and a bright red silk scarf came from his mouth. He pulled on it and a yellow one appeared next, then a green, a blue, an orange. The clown kept pulling, the colors repeating, until a pile of scarves lay curled at his feet. Mikey thought the clown must have been filled with scarves, that they were coiled up inside him.

He did bring back a program and some cotton candy for Dennis. The candy hardened, though, and Dennis was not at school next Monday anyway. When he finally did show up later that week, he wouldn't walk home with Mikey, and he refused the program. He took off running.

Mrs. Taylor worried about him, but she rarely saw him. Now here he was knocking down Dorene in his rush to get out of the Red Store.

She bought her bread quickly. She wanted to catch up with the boy before he headed for home. This was why her son was calling to him through the weeds in the field while he was eating stolen bologna.

Dennis would not answer. He thought Mrs. Taylor might try to take him back to the Red Store. He wouldn't go back. He would never go there again. He would go up to Ridge Road, to the A & P. He would go up Steelawanna Avenue. He would get up the courage to cross all those streets.

"Ma, he gone," Mikey said.

"I guess so, but it don't seem like he could get 'cross the field that quick. Let's get on home. Ya'll daddy be home soon."

And they walked on, leaving the hungry boy lost among the weeds.

10

UNVEILING

BECAUSE Venita was childless she thought she could make herself invisible. She cloaked herself in her sorrow, in her emptiness. Thinking herself unseen, she walked through All-Bright Court watching the children openly. She and Moses had been trying to have a child since they were married, three years.

At first she thought she might just be stupid, that she simply did not know what she was doing. She did not know how to call a baby, so none would come. As a girl she had been stupid about babies. Up until she was thirteen Venita thought babies came from cabbage patches.

Even though her parents grew cabbages in their garden and she never saw a baby there, she continued believing that was where they came from. She looked under the tender leaves of the young plants and between the waxy leaves of the older ones. When she was seven she pulled up an entire row of young plants, one after another she pulled them from the loamy soil, liking the sound when she pulled them, the soft ripping as the roots let go of the earth. Secrets were here. Each time she pulled up a plant she looked to see if a baby was there, a tiny head or maybe a tiny hand or foot buried in the warm soil. Her mother did not see her until she had pulled up the whole row, and then her mother ran screaming from the house. Venita did not connect the screaming with herself and what she was doing. She jumped up to see what was wrong, and when her mother got to her, she knocked her to the ground. "Girl, you done lost your mind?"

Venita was going to answer, but her mother had smacked the air out of her. Her breath flew out of her mouth like a bird. It flew from the garden while she lay on the ground, trying to weather the storm of her mother's fury.

When Venita was thirteen she had the chance to find out where babies came from. She was asked to stay home when the time came for her mother to have a baby. The other times, she and the other children had been sent to their Aunt Hattie's or Aunt Thelma's. Her mother's sister Hattie came, and so did a midwife. They had her father take the kitchen table into her parents' bedroom. From dawn until well into the night the women walked calmly through the house, in and out of the bedroom. Drinking coffee, eating spoon bread and butter beans. Her father was out on the porch, and a group of his friends had gathered. They sat drinking and smoking and playing dominoes. They played even in the darkness, by the light of a kerosene lamp. Sometimes moans came from the bedroom, but her mother did not yell out. Venita was either ignored or in the way. Feeling no sense of purpose, she wandered out into the garden.

It was late, and the ground was frozen. A blue and cold dampness was in the air. The air clung to her, made her breath appear before her, a series of diminutive clouds drifting off into the night. Venita felt like crying. She was cold and scared, wearing one of her father's old sweaters. And not only that, there were no cabbages. Where was a baby going to come from? How could a baby push through the petrified earth even if there were a cabbage? She did not even hear her aunt calling her at first.

"Venita. Ve-ni-ta. Come here, you silly gal."

She ran into the house and her aunt told her to bring her mother some water. Hattie met her at the bedroom door. Venita could not see much beyond her in the dim light of the bedroom, but she could see her mother was unconscious and sweating on the table. Venita thought she was dead, but then she saw her mother stir, and heard her moan. She noticed the blood, hiding in the folds of sheets. Venita was frozen there. Her feet were cold. She wanted to watch but was grateful when Hattie pushed her aside and shut the door. She wandered out to the porch and sat with the men.

They were drinking some peach wine her mother had put up. Her father gave her a splash in a tin cup. It was hot and sweet.

"Is your mama fenna have the baby?" her father asked.

"I don't know."

"What your aunt-nem doing in there?"

"I don't know."

"What you mean, you don't know? What you was doing in there?"

Venita began crying, puffing out enough clouds to fill a stormy sky. Her father calmed her down, filled her cup with wine. "Huh," he said. It was an apology.

She cried softly and drank the wine. Her father went back to his game, slamming dominoes down on the plank porch. Venita did not notice her hands were numb.

Morning was coming. A grayness was pushing its way

into the sky when a cry came from the house. It woke Venita where she had fallen asleep on the porch. She went inside to find her father in the kitchen. The women made him wait before they would let him in to see the baby.

Venita went in with him. It was a boy, and there he was with her mother. They were in the bed. Her mother was asleep, her hair gone back and drawn up tightly on her head. The midwife handed her father a sack and told him to take it out back and bury it.

Venita thought he was taking it to the garden, and she headed in that direction.

"Where you going?" her father asked. "Come on."

He led her to the back corner of the yard and beat at the earth with a spade. It broke in big chunks, yielding a small, shallow hole.

"It probably ain't deep enough," he said. He placed the sack in the ground and pressed the clods back into the hole.

"What's in the croaker sack?" Venita asked.

"The afterbirth. Let's go."

Venita did not ask for any more of an explanation. She went inside and up to bed. As she was falling to sleep, she thought that this was what it must feel like to be old. Stiff and tired, wanting nothing but rest and feeling like all that came before was a confusing dream.

No, it was not because she was stupid that she had no children. Venita figured even stupid women could have children — plenty had. If she wasn't stupid, maybe she was just unblessed. Unblessed wasn't the same as cursed. It was not that she had offended God.

There was a lady back home who had. She would wander through town mumbling, her hair matted like a sheep's coat, her clothes tattered, carrying a dirty rubber doll wrapped in a threadbare diaper. Venita's mother told her about the woman.

"That woman cursed. When her was a girl no bigger than you, her family-nem had a cat that had kittens. They needed that cat to keep mice out the house, but they ain't need no litter of kittens to feed. Her family-nem couldn't afford it. So the mama tied them up in a sack and told her to take it down to the creek and throw it in. There ain't no sin in that, 'cause the Lord understand. He know how much you can bear. He would lift they soul up right out the water. Pluck they soul out.

"But that girl was a regular hardhead, had a head like a regular rock. She thought her mama was being mean, so her took it in her head to be mean too. Before her got to the creek her threw the sack in a trash can that was on fire.

"Them cats was screaming and yelling to get out the bag. Now, her family-nem didn't find out 'bout it then. But when her grew up it all come out. Ain't nothing you can't do in the dark that don't come out in the light. When her grew up and took a husband, her ain't had no one baby. Her had a whole litter, five or six, all born at the same time. All born live, too, and crying just like them kittens. Every last one died. Her told her family-nem. Her was raving. All 'bout kittens and a fire. They say her was in shock, you know. Her ain't never come out it.

"The Lord dried her womb up, turned her womb into a barren field. That's the way of the Lord."

Venita had never done anything that would cause God to curse her. But how could the women in All-Bright Court know that? All they could know was her emptiness. So she tried to hide from them in broad daylight, to make herself invisible while she was hanging clothes, shopping, sitting on the porch. She longed to know one of the women.

Venita was not invisible. Mary Kate had seen her, so bold-faced, looking at her, at her children. Mary Kate knew she looked at the children because she was empty, but Mary Kate did not know Venita looked at her because she was lonely. Mary Kate had never taken out time to consider that possibility. In the nearly four years since Venita moved in, she had never said more than "hey" to Venita.

Four years had filled up quickly. Four years of diapers and sheets and work clothes strung on lines. Up until '65 she had a wringer washer. She had four years of sprinkling, starching, ironing. Four years of grits, redeye gravy, beaten biscuits, fried porgies, fried chicken, fried tomatoes, fried corn, fried pork chops, smothered pork chops, field peas, black-eyed peas, corn bread. Four years of scrubbing the floors, the children, the walls, the dishes, the toilet, the tub. Four years of making love, rocking babies, changing diapers. And not just these four years, but the six years of her married life had been spent taking care of everyone else, of everything else. She had never had the time to contemplate her own loneliness, or anyone else's. And if you had asked her, she would have thought she had said more than "hey" to Venita. She would have thought she knew her. She had never taken out the time to notice that whenever she spoke to Venita, Venita looked shocked.

It was Samuel who challenged what she knew. He challenged who she thought she was, and she took his challenge as a threat.

It was another dismal Saturday in the dead of winter, and the weather had been so bad that Samuel had not seen the sun in more than a month. He and Mary Kate and the children were watching television, and he was already in a bad mood because Mary Kate wanted to see *Mission: Impossible* instead of *Get Smart*. *Mission: Impossible* had a black person in it. Samuel had told her, "I don't want to see no Negro sweat for a hour. That's all they let him do. He always be crawling under stuff, fixing it. He ain't nothing but a handyman." Mary Kate didn't say anything. She was holding the baby Mary. But he put his foot down when she wanted to watch *The Hollywood Palace* because Sammy Davis Jr. was going to be on.

"That Tom!" he yelled.

"He not no Tom," she said.

"He is. What he going be doing? Bowing and scraping and shining shoes. A big smile and tap dancing like a black monkey on a string. That's what he going be doing."

"He help Dr. King, you know that, working for our rights. You just jealous. He making big money."

"I'm not jealous. I think he putting on a act. He don't care nothing 'bout Negroes, marrying that white woman. I see Negroes like him every day, breaking into a goddamn buck-and-wing every time a white man come by. I can't stand to see a Negro act like that. You want to see our son grow up and be like that?"

"Me?" Mikey asked.

"Yeah, you. What other son I got? Don't you grow up and be no white man's nigger, hear me?"

"Samuel, stop talking like that."

"Like what? You need to get out in the world. All you do is set in the house and keep to yourself."

"You think all I do is set here all day? Who you think look after your kids, clean the house, wash—"

"That ain't what I'm saying. I know you do all that, but you don't know nobody. You ain't got one girlfriend. Tell me that you do," Samuel said.

"How many friends *you* got? Who you bring 'round here?"

"Most of them rumheads I know I wouldn't bring 'round you and the kids. You know I go out, play some cards, go to the diner sometime, to the hall. You don't do nothing."

"I be tired. Don't you think I be tired?" Mary Kate asked.

"I ain't saying you not tired. I'm saying I'm starting to think you hankty."

"You going sit there and call me stuck-up in front my kids?" She felt fire in her throat and jumped from her chair. She had been holding Mary on her lap. The baby rolled onto the floor and started crying. The baby's fear spread to the other children and they began yelling.

Mary Kate circled Samuel's chair. "Hankty, hankty, hankty," she said over and over, her voice getting higher and higher each time she said the word. She came to a stop in front of his chair. Samuel was scared. It was like he poured water on a wildcat. She looked as if she were going to scratch him to death.

"The baby," he said. "Look at the baby."

She did not look.

"It ain't me that said it. I just heard it said."

"Who said it?" she pressed.

"You know how Negroes talk."

"Who said it?" she asked.

"I don't know. You know Negroes always talking, always got to have something to say. That's our problem. We talk too much."

"I don't know 'bout 'we.' You don't know when to shut up," Mary Kate said.

"I'm shutting up right 'bout now," Samuel said.

"Well, you should," she said. She picked the baby up from the floor. Samuel grabbed Mary Kate and pulled her onto his lap.

"Don't you be trying to make up to me." She began patting the baby gently on the back. "And what ya'll was screaming for?" she said to Mikey and Dorene. "Ya'll little pitchers got big ears."

"What that mean?" Mikey asked.

"That mean don't be minding grown folks' business. Hollering like ya'll crazy."

"Let's put the kids to bed now," Samuel whispered.

Mary Kate got up from his lap. "What you going to go and ask a hankty woman that for?"

"Come on, baby. Let it die."

"So, now I'm your baby?"

"Yeah. You know that," Samuel said.

"Samuel, do you really think I'm hankty?" she asked. She was serious.

Samuel looked at her. "Naw. I told you I never said it. I say you keep to yourself too much. I'm a stand by that. You can be mad at me if you want to. It's the truth. You need to get out, make you some girlfriends for your own good."

"I'm not mad," Mary Kate said. "Dorene and Mikey, ya'll go on upstairs."

"What about the baby?" Mikey asked.

"Don't worry 'bout her. You do what your mama say," Samuel said.

Mary Kate went and sat back down on Samuel's lap. "You know," she said to Samuel, "putting the kids to bed and going upstairs with you is how I stay in trouble."

"It ain't trouble. I'm your husband. We going to have a boy this time. I can feel it. You carrying a boy."

In the last few days of winter, when warmth was beginning to push its way up through the earth, Mary Kate took on Samuel's challenge. She had stopped in the Red Store with Dorene and Mary, and Venita was at the counter. Mr.

Jablonski was weighing a piece of salt pork for her. At first, she walked past Venita like she did not see her, leaving Venita to feel secure in her guise of invisibility.

Venita was staring at Dorene. Dorene had taken off the woolen scarf that covered her head. Her hair was greased and parted into a series of interconnected braids that ran off the back of her head. To Venita, her hair looked like a newly planted spring field.

Mary Kate saw Venita staring at Dorene, and said, "That pork any good?"

Venita started. She was being summoned from her hiding place.

"Of course the pork is good. You know my meat is always good," Mr. Jablonski said.

"I was talking to her," Mary Kate said, nodding her head toward Venita. "I figure she know more 'bout salt meat than you."

Venita heard herself say, "It's awful fat."

"What do you expect?" Mr. Jablonski said. "It's pork we're talking here."

"My husband like it fat," Mary Kate said, ignoring him. "How your husband like it?"

"He like it fat. He partial to fatback, but there ain't none today."

"Tuesday," Mr. Jablonski said. "I'll have some in on Tuesday, and I'll have some tripe and pigs' feet."

Mary Kate left the girls at the counter and went to the back of the store. Venita looked at them. "How ya'll?" she asked. They both stared at her. Mary could not talk, and Dorene was too shy to speak. Their silence made Venita momentarily disappear.

"You heard the woman speak, Dorene. You speak when grown folks speak to you," Mary Kate said, returning to the counter. She had two boxes of starch.

"Hello," Dorene said.

"'Hello' what?" Mary Kate prompted.

"Hello, ma'am."

"You know how it be with kids," Mary Kate said. "You got to learn 'em while they young."

Venita was silent.

Both of the women signed Mr. Jablonski's green ledger. Before they left the store, Mary Kate tied the scarf on Dorene's head.

"Your name Ventrice, right?"

"My name Venita."

"My name Mary Kate, Mary Kate Taylor. My girls' names Dorene and Mary."

Venita walked along beside Mary Kate and the girls, feeling giddy. It was like being found at hide and seek, lurking in the dark behind a bush. It was as if you had dissolved into the bush, folded yourself into leaves, stretched yourself into branches, and now that you were found, were turning yourself human again, warm and water-laden and briny. Running, laughing through the shadows, dodging your pursuer, racing for the safety of home. But as Venita walked, as she, Mary Kate, and the girls crossed the field, she realized she did not want to go home. She was glad they were walking slowly. Mary Kate could not walk quickly. She was carrying the baby low.

They came to Mary Kate's row first, and Venita hesitated. Mary Kate could see her reticence. "I got to be getting home. My boy coming home for lunch, and I got to get dinner started."

"Me too," Venita said. "I mean, cooking for my husband. He on days now." She stood facing Mary Kate and began backing away.

"Come 'round sometime, hear? I be having some time to visit after lunch."

Venita did not answer. She broke into a run.

Mary Kate was going to tell Samuel about her, about the way people could be. See, she wanted to say, people crazy. You go all out your way, and they run off like something after them. I'm not going be putting myself out. People can call me what they want to.

It was a good thing she did not say anything, because Venita did visit. It was nearly two weeks later. While Mary Kate was out in the back yard hanging up clothes, Venita came around the corner carrying a brown paper bag. She was turning to go back home when Mary Kate saw her.

"Hey."

"Hey," Venita said. "I was going to stop by, but I see you busy."

"I'm not busy. This my last load, come on."

The girls were asleep, and Venita and Mary Kate sat in the living room. Venita had brought over a pound cake, a small golden loaf, which she offered to Mary Kate.

"This just the thing for my sweet tooth. It seem like when you carrying, you be having a taste for all kind of things."

Mary Kate ate four slices of cake. She ate on the move, checking pots on the stove, looking in on the girls, folding clothes. All the while she moved with a slow and gentle grace.

To Venita it seemed the baby was not a visitor to her body but a natural part of it. "You never get tired, do you?"

"I be tired all the time," Mary Kate said. "Don't pay no mind to me."

"You never sit down," Venita said. "Excuse me for saying that. It probably ain't my place. I ain't mean nothing by it."

"Yes, you did," Mary Kate said, and she laughed. "You sound like my doctor. He want me to set down and take it easy. But if I don't do, who going to do?"

"Nobody," Venita offered.

"That's what I say, talking 'bout take it easy. That's what my doctor say, like *he* know. When my husband come home from work, he want to eat. He need clean clothes to wear. You know how dirty them work clothes be. My baby need clean diapers. I got to send my boy off to school. Tell me, who going to do?"

"Nobody," Venita said.

"That's what I say."

At dinner that night Mary Kate brought up the visit. "I had me a visitor this afternoon," she teased.

"I know. I saw him tripping out the back door when I came in," Samuel said.

"Samuel!"

"Who?" Mikey asked. "Who was here?"

"It was Miz Reed — and you mind your own business, boy. Samuel, why you stirring stink?" Her voice was rising.

"I'm not stirring stink. I'm happy to hear you had company."

"You know her husband?"

"Humph."

"What's that supposed to mean? You know him?"

"Yeah, I know Moses. He a T-o-m," Samuel said.

"That spell Tom," Mikey said.

Mary Kate swatted at him from across the table. "How many times I got to tell you to not be minding grown folks' business."

"I don't know her," Samuel said. "But I know she barren."

"How you know?" Mary Kate asked.

"I just know. You know how Negroes talk."

Venita would come by on Monday and Wednesday afternoons and, sitting surrounded by piles of clean clothes, help Mary Kate eat her way through the end of her last trimester. They ate pound cake, bread pudding, jelly cake, rice pudding, anything that was sweet and homemade. Venita turned out dessert after dessert. She gained weight. Being there with Mary Kate made her feel pregnant. Her face filled in and her stomach rounded out.

Mary Kate would top off each dessert with a handful of starch. If the girls were up, they would beg for some.

"I eat so much of this stuff that it constipate me," Mary Kate told Venita one afternoon.

"Why you eat it, then?" Venita asked.

"There really ain't no why. I just crave it. You know how it is when you expecting. You be —" Mary Kate stopped talking and filled her mouth with starch. "When women expecting, they crave all sorts of things. Glodene —"

"Who Glodene?"

"She Isaac mama, that crazy boy mama. Heard say Glodene got to craving for some dirt so bad one time she dug outside her back door and tried to eat some of that. She wasn't down home, either. She was right over in Buffalo, trying to eat Buffalo dirt. Can you beat that?" Mary Kate said.

"Pass me the box," Venita said. She poured some starch in her mouth. A little cloud of dust rose from the box and choked her, causing her to spit the starch out. It sprayed out onto the couch, the floor. Mary Kate got up to clean it.

"Let me," Venita said. She was so embarrassed. If she could have, she would have disappeared. But she had forgotten how.

"Pour some in your hand," Mary Kate said.

"Naw, I shouldn't."

"Go 'head, girl," Mary Kate said.

Venita picked up the blue and white box and carefully poured a few pieces into her hand. It tasted like nothing, and left her mouth feeling pasty and dry. "I see how you can crave it. It's good," she lied, licking the film from the roof of her mouth.

"You think so? If the truth be told, I don't like it. I just crave for it."

Going home was hard. Mikey's return from school signaled it was time for her to leave. Each woman had work to do, corn bread to bake, pots to reheat. For Venita, every parting was like a little death. She went home and her house was empty. She and Moses ate their dinner in silence. She had told him about Mary Kate: "You know that woman with all them kids?"

"That describe half the women 'round here," he said.

"She nice," Venita said. "She my friend."

"A woman with a house of kids don't need no friends. How she got time to visit with you?"

"She find time," Venita said. "She my friend."

"She need a friend like she need a hole in the head."

Venita did not press the issue. On that night, like on so many others, she made passionless love to him. She had no room for passion. She was filled up with purpose. She would have a baby.

But what Moses said had stuck in her mind. Mary Kate *was* her friend. How could he even question? Like a hole in the head.

If the truth be told, Mary Kate looked forward to seeing Venita too. She found herself saving up things to say to her, storing them away in her mind, folding them as neatly as sheets. On the days that Venita did not come over, when the house was quiet, the girls sleeping, Mikey at school, Samuel working, the sheets would sometimes come unfolded, all by themselves. Under their own volition they would come billowing down into the house. She would look up from chopping onions, from ironing a shirt, from scrubbing a floor, and realize the wave that was rolling lazily through the house was the sound of her own voice. The words slipped out of her mind. She would stop herself then, sometimes turn on *Search for Tomorrow*. What if someone came to the door and heard her talking? People would think she was crazy.

On the days Venita did not come, Mary Kate missed her. That was the word for it. Missed. She did not tell Samuel this, but rather lived uneasily with the silences that were punctuated by the sudden fluttering of her voice.

She was becoming acquainted with loneliness. Mary Kate was learning about loneliness from a woman who was newly visible, though Venita brought little of herself when she came; she often only sat and ate and nodded. It seemed that Venita was content with merely being there, that there was nothing left to be said. Both women knew it was not true.

Her barrenness stood between them, a vast and unexplored field. It defined the path they took, a path that was roundabout and safe. Venita did not mention it. Though she was sure that everyone knew, she would not run the risk of putting her business in the street. One does not come into existence to be dismissed as trash. She did not want to tell it, and Mary Kate did not want to ask. This was a game adults played — minding your own business.

If a woman had a husband who beat her to water every night, and her neighbors heard her screaming, if they heard her running down the walls, it was nobody's business. The real test would come the next day. If the woman was seen hanging out clothes, anyone who had heard her cries would quickly look away, would pretend not to see her. These people lived inches away from one another, and much of what was done did not have to be told. They did not look away because they did not want to know. They looked away because they *did* know, and looking away was the only way to grant the woman dignity, to go on believing, to let her go on believing she was a woman.

A week before Mary Kate's baby was due, Venita had a dream. To these people who had followed the highways from the South, who had come from the cotton fields, the cane fields, the fields of rivers of rice, dreams were powerful. To them, waking life did not inform dream life. Dream life informed waking life. Dream life was filled with winged harbingers that swooped into waking life carrying messages that should not be ignored. Daytime dreams, waking dreams, were especially filled with harbingers. During the day, one was trespassing in dream life and was liable to be chased into wakefulness by something that was better left unknown.

Venita, while trying to rest her eyes before going to Mary Kate's, was swept into a waking dream. It was a winter night, and instead of grass there were cabbages in her back yard. Someone had forgotten to harvest them. Their growth stunted, they were gnarled fists, and Venita pulled at them, trying to uproot them, trying to feel that delicious ripping move through her body, taste the flavor of it in her mouth. But the plants were stuck to the ground. She hacked at them with a hoe, but instead of ripping free, the heads broke off cleanly and rolled through the yard. When she finished lopping the heads off from an entire row, she heard a noise coming from the beginning of the row. Venita thought she was hearing things, but the noise was clear.

When she reached the beginning of the row it was daylight, and there was a baby where she had dug up the first cabbage. The baby was emerging from the darkness, white, colorless, struggling to reach the light. Venita pulled the baby out by a wrist. It did not tear from the ground, but slipped noiselessly into the world. The baby was a girl, and Venita placed her on the ground while she looked for something to wrap her in.

She found nothing. All the cabbages had disappeared. She returned to the baby only to see her slipping away. Something was pulling her, and while Venita ran toward her, shouting, the baby sank quietly into the earth.

The sound of Venita's own screaming awoke her. She jumped from the couch like it was afire. She was so happy to be awake, to be dropped from the heights of her dream to the safety of her living room, that she felt like crying.

She smelled smoke in the house. Venita ran to the kitchen to discover the pan of bread pudding she left baking in the stove had burned up. She had slept for almost an hour.

Someone was knocking at her front door, and it couldn't have been a worse time. All she wanted to do was get to Mary Kate's.

It was Mary Kate. She stood on the steps with Mary wrapped in a blanket and Dorene at her side. "I was worried 'bout you, you not showing up and all."

Venita stared at them. She was so surprised that she did not think to ask them in. "I fell asleep. I was just resting my eyes for a minute, just one minute —"

"What's burning?"

"That's my bread pudding, burned blacker than a hat." She asked Mary Kate and the girls to come in. "Pardon my manners," she said. "You must think I ain't had no upbringing. Come on in."

Venita was excited to have visitors. It was the first company she had ever had in her house. But she was too distracted to show how pleased she was. She was trying to push the darkness of the dream from her mind, to make her mind a blue and blank sky. But the darkness formed itself into a cloud that filled her thoughts.

She had her company sit in the living room among the starched doilies, the cut-glass ashtrays, the figurines of dogs and cats. In the kitchen, Venita tried to scrape the bread pudding from the pan. It all came out except for about an inch that was stuck fast.

"You don't have to do that now," Mary Kate said, slapping the girls' hands away from the ashtrays. "Come on and set."

Venita did not answer. She wanted to. She wanted to come and sit, but she could not move. The cloud in her mind was producing flash after flash of memory. A storm was swirling through her mind, and the water from it spilled out of the holes in her head. She cried quietly, and Mary Kate was drawn to her silence.

She left the girls in the living room and went to the kitchen. When she saw Venita there, crying and scraping away at the pan, she stopped. This was none of her business. She was going to turn and leave when Venita looked up.

Her eyes were a bruised pink, the color of the crushed petals of a damask rose. In her eyes, mixed right in with the blemished rose color, was a question she had been formulating even in her days of invisibility, a question that she was looking for Mary Kate to answer. But the first words that came to her were "I'm all right."

"Why you crying? You crying for something."

"Nothing," Venita said, and she added, "I had a dream."

She told Mary Kate about her dream, and while she talked she scraped the pan. Venita stopped crying while she told it, but when she came to the end, she started crying again.

"Me and Moses ain't never going to have children."

And so here it was. The field that stood between them, so vast and unexplored, reduced to a short walk across a kitchen floor.

"You don't know that," Mary Kate said as she walked to where Venita stood. "Ain't no way of knowing that," she said, patting Venita on the back just the way she would have patted a baby.

Mary Kate was not convinced of the truth of what she had said. She had said it the way you tell a child, "Don't be scared of the dark. Ain't nothing in the dark going to hurt you." She said it like a well-intended lie. Because you could tell your child not to be afraid of the dark and know there was a world of fear there.

Once when she was home alone at night, when she had only Dorene and Mikey, Mikey came to her. He had heard a noise downstairs. Samuel was pulling some nights so there would be extra money for Christmas, so she had to go investigate the noise. In her sleepy state she got up and tiptoed down the stairs, Mikey at her heels. From the bottom of the stairs she saw the shadow of a man standing in the kitchen. She screamed. Mikey screamed, and they both ran up the stairs. Mikey dove in the bed with her.

"What was it, Mama?"

"What you think it was? Shush now."

She told Samuel about it the next morning. "That wasn't nothing but my work clothes throwed 'cross a hanger."

"No they wasn't. That's what them clothes want you to think. Some kind of haint was what it was. Mikey saw it too."

"What you see, son?"

"I don't know," he said. "Mama saw something."

"Mama saw something? *Mama* saw something?" The

pitch of her voice was rising. "He the one woke *me* up. Talking 'bout *he* heard something. Talking 'bout *Mama* saw something. Spent the whole night clinging to me like a little monkey. Had to peel him off my back this morning."

"You got to stop worrying," Mary Kate said now to Venita. "The Lord going to bless you. He got something good planned for you."

"You really think so?" Venita asked. She was calmer. The storm inside her was blowing over.

"Look what he did for Sarah."

"Who Sarah? She live 'round here?" Venita asked. Just then they heard a crash in the living room.

"Something broke," Dorene called out.

"Something broke, my foot. What you done touched I asked you to let 'lone?" Mary Kate said. "Come on in here and bring the baby."

Dorene appeared at the kitchen door holding a squirming Mary. "It ain't enough you girls make a mess at home, but you to come to somebody else house tearing up. I'm a whip you."

"Don't do that," Venita said. "Come here," she said to Dorene. "I'm a clean up the mess. It ain't nothing but a accident, right baby?"

Dorene nodded her head, and when she caught her mother looking at her, added, "Yes, ma'am."

Venita sat down on a kitchen chair and pulled Dorene up on her lap. "What you was saying 'bout Sarah?"

"Sarah from the Bible," Mary Kate said, and eased herself down on a chair. Mary climbed into her lap. "The Lord blessed her."

Venita remembered the story. The Lord had opened up her womb when she was an old woman. "You think he can do it for me?"

"He got something good planned for you."

Venita smiled and hugged Dorene close to her.

"I got a taste for something sweet," Mary Kate said. "I got some corn bread at home. We could have that with some Alaga. Would you like that?" she asked Venita.

"I would. I ain't had bread and syrup in a long while, since I came north."

"My mama call it a hard-time dessert, but it's all I got."

On the walk over to Mary Kate's, Venita couldn't help smiling. Mary Kate was blessed. She must know. There was no need to worry. Mary Kate *had* to know.

If the truth be told, Mary Kate did not know. All she knew was that when she lay with her husband she came up pregnant. Her mother had told her that. "You lay down with a man, you come up with a baby." It was just that simple.

Venita knew this. She knew babies did not come from cabbage patches, but from men. But what Venita did not think of, what she had never thought of, was going to a doctor. There was nothing a doctor could do. He could not give her a baby. All there was for her to do was wait. When it was time, a child would come to her.

11

EXTINGUISHED

HENRY HAD come back from Vietnam with a scarred face. It looked like melted plastic. It was shiny and the skin was thick. Half of his hair had been burned away. Some of the children called him Halloween.

Samuel talked to him in the Red Store a week after he returned. "I hear it was napalm."

"Yeah, it was. It came from a flame thrower. I never knew what hit me," Henry said. "I found out when I was in the hospital."

Dorene was with her father that day. It was early evening, and as they had walked across the field to the store, a yacht of a car floated up Holbrook toward the pike.

When the car passed, Dorene began singing a song to herself. She sang it over and over until she saw Henry. In the store, while her father spoke, she hid behind him. She was too young to remember Henry's slick hair, his smooth skin. She was born the year he went to Vietnam.

Two weeks after Dorene heard Henry talking about napalm, she still hid under a blanket when the evening news came on.

Mikey watched, her parents watched, and sometimes even Mary watched. But as the black-and-white Motorola played in the living room, Dorene hid. She had to protect herself from the ugly. She did not even want to listen to news of the war. But she could still hear it in the kitchen, and she was scared to go upstairs by herself, so she lay on the couch and heard Walter Cronkite, tried not to listen to Walter Cronkite, and protected herself from the ugly. She could hear the bombs exploding and the machine guns firing in the living room. And then there was the napalm. It fell from the sky on the Vietnamese children, and it made them ugly.

Dorene knew it was white men who told these war stories. They came on every night to tell what was happening. She knew what was happening. Napalm was being dropped on some little, stupid Vietnamese children. Dorene thought Vietnam was probably close. Maybe you could get there on a bus. She was afraid war would come to All-Bright Court. She was afraid a white man would come here and tell war stories, that her mother would be seen on television, running down the street holding her limp, ugly body.

For the last two weeks while Dorene lay hidden under her blanket, listening and not listening, peeking when she dared, Newark and Detroit had burned. Sixty-six people were killed. Dorene pushed events together, the sirens, the looting, the men in uniforms, the white reporters, the talk of angry Negroes. Everything was one.

While Mikey and Mary played with the baby Olivia, their mother would say, "Unh, unh, unh" or "Will you look at that, Samuel. Negroes done gone crazy. This don't make no sense."

He did not answer. Once, Dorene peered out, expecting her father to be asleep, expecting her mother to be talking to the walls. But her father was awake, sitting on the edge of his chair. He looked as if he were about to cry.

On this night, again, Dorene was ready for the war. Before the news started, she asked softly from under the blanket, "Daddy, do napalm make you ugly?"

"No, Little Bit, it kill you," her father said.

"You sure it don't make you ugly?"

"I told you, it kill you. What make you think it make you ugly?"

"'Cause it didn't kill Henry. It made him ugly," Dorene said. "He say napalm fell on him. Didn't he used to have a face, Daddy?"

"Sure, he had a face. He still got one."

"No he don't. He got a Halloween mask," Mikey said.

"Don't say things like that," Mrs. Taylor said.

"It's true," Mikey said. "All the kids be calling him that."

"Well, don't you be calling him that. If I hear you call Henry out his name, I'm a beat your ass," Mr. Taylor said.

"How napalm make Henry ugly?" Dorene asked.

"He got burned. That stuff burned him. Henry like to died in Vietnam."

"I never seen him on the news, Daddy. Why wasn't he on the news?"

"They don't be showing the whole war on the news. If they did, it would be all they showed. The war go on day and night."

Dorene asked, "They going drop napalm here?"

"Naw. Vietnam way on the other side of the world. There won't be no war here. We safe here."

And Dorene came out from under her blanket. She went and sat on her father's lap. She didn't open her eyes while the war was on. Before it was over, her father's eyes were closed too.

12

BROODING

"YOU DONE turned white, and you can't stay here. You got to go live with white folks," Mikey's father told him.

"But Daddy, let me tell you —"

"Don't 'but' me, boy. You ain't got nothing to tell me that I want to hear." With this, he pushed Mikey out the front door. It was snowing, and as Mikey tumbled into the yard he saw his arms, his legs. He was white. Dressed only in his underwear, he jumped up and headed toward the house. He would die out here. He would die. Didn't his father know that? He must know. Mikey had to get back inside before he froze, but the house was gone, and he heard laughter.

Mikey ran toward it and found Cheryl. She was laughing at him from an upstairs window. The entire first floor of the building was bricked up, no windows, no door. There was not even a porch.

"What do you want, smarty?" she asked.

"Let me in," Mikey pleaded.

It had stopped snowing, and a rope dropped from the

window. When Mikey tried to pull himself up, he couldn't. The rope was greased. Cheryl laughed, and the rope jerked from his hands so hard that it burned him.

"Adiós!" she said.

Mikey fell, picked himself up, and saw his arms, his legs. He was black, and he reached for the rope again. It disappeared from the window. Cheryl disappeared from the window. Then the window disappeared, filling in brick by brick.

Mikey started for home. It was snowing again, and he was lost. There was nothing around him except a nebulous, cold whiteness. He thought of giving up and saw himself lying down.

He had died, but he was not dead. There were two of him. A white him was lying on the ground, being rapidly covered with snow. The black him was watching. He had to get home to tell his father he was dead. The way it was snowing no one would ever find him, and his mother would never know what had become of him.

"Mama, mama," he yelled, but his yell came out as barely a whisper. The wind was reaching into his mouth, taking his voice away.

"Mama, mama," he whispered, and was surprised to hear the sound of his voice rippling through the darkness of his room. He was glad that his voice had been soft. If he had yelled, his mother would have come to him, and he did not know what he would have told her. He could not tell her that *it* had happened, that everything had to do with Cheryl, the Chug-a-lug, even though the Chug-a-lugs had come and gone. They had been gone for more than two weeks.

During the spring, the Zakrezewski family had moved into 24, the apartment at the end of the row where the Taylors lived. No white family had moved in in nearly four years, and their arrival seemed strange. The white flight was nearly complete. When the Zakrezewskis moved in, only two white families remained. They both lived on the very last row, right next door to each other. They spoke to their neighbors when coming or going, or upon seeing them on the street. Other than that, they were quiet and kept to themselves. To their neighbors this made them respectable. But right away the Zakrezewskis seemed different.

They had no upper lips. Not one member of the family had one. This made their faces seem unbalanced, overly long. But when the children sang about the Zakrezewskis, they made no mention of their lips.

The children nicknamed them the Chug-a-lugs, and they made up a rhyme about them:

> Three skinny bennies
> And two fat tubs,
> We call 'em the Chug-a-lugs.

The rhyme had only this one verse, which was sung over and over. It was the kind of song that seemed not to have been started by any one child, but in the cool, dry, windy summer of 1967, all of the children knew it. This one verse was blown on the wind, and the children sang about the Chug-a-lugs like they sang about Sally Walker, Miss Sue, Miss Mary Mack. The song was never sung directly to any of the family members. It was sung when one of them was spotted around All-Bright Court. If the Zakrezewskis had listened closely, they probably could have figured out they were the Chug-a-lugs.

All the males, the father and the two boys, were very thin. Their pants rode halfway down their behinds. They were the skinny bennies. The females were fat, the mother and daughter. The two fat tubs. They were the kind of females who looked pregnant, and always would look pregnant, no matter their ages.

The little girl, Cheryl, was only seven, and she looked like a pregnant child. She was a twin, but the only way she and her brother Chris resembled each other was that they didn't have upper lips. Cheryl claimed she and Chris were identical twins who did not look alike, and they were the only set of identical twins in the world who were a boy and a girl. And not only that, she said; her name was Chris too. They were Chris and Chris, but everyone in her family called her Cheryl so they wouldn't get them mixed up.

Mikey asked his mother about it.

"That white girl was pulling your leg. Only two boys or two girls can be identical."

"How come?" Mikey asked.

"That's the way things is. That's the way babies come."

"Come from where? Where babies come from?"

"Heaven," his mother said.

"Really, Mama? How they get from way up there?" he asked, pointing at the ceiling.

"Storks."

"I never saw no stork 'round her," Mikey said.

"Why you got to question everything, boy?"

"But Mama, Cheryl say she and Chris identical—"

"And she told you her name was Chris too. And another thing. She shouldn't be putting her family business out in the street, even if it's a story. That's trashy. That's what trash do."

This was why the adults were wary of the Chug-a-lug clan. They put their business in the street, told their business in front of other people. A child running around telling anyone who was willing to listen that she was a two-sex non-look-alike identical twin who was going under an alias was a child who had no upbringing.

Mikey confronted Cheryl about her story, but she would not discuss it with him. Instead, she asked him a question. "Which came first, the chicken or the egg?"

Mikey could not believe how simple the question was. "The chicken," he blurted out.

"Well, if you're so smart, where did the chicken come from?"

"A egg," Mikey said.

"Aha!" Cheryl said. "You said the chicken came first."

Mikey was stunned.

"You don't know where the chicken came from, do you, smarty?"

That night when he was in the tub he thought about it, pressing his eyelids together tightly, turning eggs into chickens, chickens into eggs. The answer would not come to him, and that bothered him. Mikey liked knowing about things, how they happened, how they worked.

His father came into the bathroom. "Boy, if you stay in that tub any longer, you going to turn white."

"For real?"

"Yeah, for real. Then me and your mama will have to send you off to live with some white folks. You couldn't stay here with us."

Mikey looked down at himself. "For real, Daddy?" he asked, his eyes getting big.

His father laughed. "No, not for real. Can't you tell when somebody's pulling your leg? You need to get out the tub. The water getting cold, and you know your sisters got to get in here."

Mikey stood up and began washing himself. "Daddy, which came first, the chicken or the egg?"

"The chicken."

"Aha!" Mikey yelled. "Well, where the chicken come from?" Mikey asked. He could not help giggling.

"God," his father said. "Clean your neck."

Mikey stood there holding his washcloth. He hadn't planned on this. Cheryl had not mentioned anything about God.

"Clean your neck, or do you want you mother to come in here and wash it?"

Mikey began scrubbing again. "Well, where God come from?"

"He always was and always will be."

"That don't make no sense, Daddy."

"What you mean, it don't make no sense? Why God got to make sense to you?" his father asked.

"But Daddy, he got to come from someplace, like the chicken. If the chicken come first, it didn't come from a egg. If a egg come first, it didn't come from a chicken . . . Where God come from?"

"I done told you, and don't be asking so many questions. You always be asking so many questions. Where you get all of 'em?"

Mikey wanted to tell him that Cheryl had asked him the chicken-and-egg question. But if he told his father, it would only be proof for him, and he could hear his father saying, Your mama done told you, that child trash.

The whole family was trash, and not one month after they blew into All-Bright Court like scraps of paper caught up in a sudden upswirl of wind, they proved it.

It was not even warm yet, but the mother and father were sitting out on the cold stone front porch, drinking Genesee beer right out of quart bottles. One of the living room windows was open, and sitting in it was a Philco radio tuned to a country-and-western station. The twang of the music from the tinny radio bounced off of the low ceiling of clouds, treating their neighbors to what seemed like an interminable night at the Grand Ole Opry.

Venita had been walking over to Mary Kate's house to take her a jar of strawberry preserves. That's the excuse she gave Moses. She really wanted to know where the music was coming from. As she walked past the Zakrezewski house, she nodded and spoke. "Good evening," she said.

They both just stared at her, the skinny husband, the fat wife. Then the husband told the wife, "Angela, get that god-damn Indian boy of yours to go over to the store and get some more beer."

That was how it was discovered that the Chug-a-lugs were not a wholly white family. Cheryl confirmed it. She seemed to be the self-appointed messenger of all the trashy goings-on in her family's life. Whatever was not evident enough by her parents' living their lives on the front porch, she made clear.

She was the one who told Mikey about her older brother. "Paulie isn't my whole brother, he's half my brother and half Indian. His daddy was a stupid Indian, a whole Indian that got drunk and drowneded himself in the lake one fall. He walked right into it and drowneded. They didn't find him until spring. The lake turned him up, and he was swole up like a balloon and half ate up by fish."

Cheryl told Mikey this, but she did not tell him that this boy was a ghost in their family. She was too young to notice that he existed only in the periphery of their vision. He haunted the shadows of their consciousness.

Paulie watched the children while Jake and Angela were at work. He sat inside, looking through the window while they played outside. Even when he was not watching them, he rarely ventured from the dimness of the house.

Isaac had heard that this boy was half Indian, and sometimes when he was over that way, he would stroll past the house and tease him. "How!" he would yell at the boy, or give him a whoop. "Woo-woo-woo-woo. Woo-woo-woo-woo." The boy would just continue staring blankly. Isaac was becoming a ghost himself. He was moving into the shadows of life, and he was going on the haunt.

The other parents did not stop their children from playing with the Chug-a-lugs. They might be trash, but they were only children. But the other parents would have stopped them from playing with the Chug-a-lugs if they had known about Chris and his dancing.

He had done his dance only three times, while his parents were at work. Each time, a group of children had gathered around one of the back windows. Cheryl stood outside with them. Paulie sat staring out the other kitchen window. Chris turned the radio on, whipped the knob down the dial to a rock station, hopped on top of the metal kitchen table, and pulled his shorts and underpants down.

Chris made sure he had the attention of all the faces gathered around, faces ash-purple like unwashed plums, all except Cheryl's. Her face was round and peachy. Then Chris began dancing, jumping up and down, twisting, spinning. It was a short, spastic dance, not even a minute. To conclude the dance, Chris would grab hold of his penis and shake it at the audience.

Mikey had been there for all three performances. When Chris would finish his dance, all the children would run to the field and release their laughter in the tangle of weeds.

It was a miracle that the mothers never found out. It was a testament to the secret lives of children.

Jake Zakrezewski paid as little attention to the twins as he could. From his day shift at Capital, he headed straight for his mistress. Chris and Cheryl could be blowing through All-Bright Court like a two-sex, non-look-alike twin tornado, and Jake would not have left his mistress's side.

He was having an affair with a '57 Pontiac. The Star Chief. She was a two-door yellow convertible. White interior. One-hundred-twenty-two-inch wheelbase. Two hundred seventy horsepower. A black racing stripe ran along each side and flared out once it passed the door. Four chrome stars shone in the blackness of each broad stripe. Chrome rockets finished off the stripes, extending back to the taillights.

Jake would make love to her for hours, washing and polishing, shining her chrome, conditioning her seats. He would lie under her jacked-up body, bend over her open hood, listening to her purr. He spent more time attending to her needs than to anyone else's in his family. Despite all the time he spent on her while she was standing still, he took her out only once a week.

On Fridays the whole family would pile into the beloved Sky Chief and go to Mexico. That was where Cheryl said they went, to Mexico by car on Friday evening. They returned the next night. This was surely a lie.

That boat of a car, that land yacht, which eased out of All-Bright Court every Friday evening and floated up Hanna, down Wilmuth, onto Holbrook, and then onto the pike, looked as if it could take them to Mexico, as if it could go out on the open sea and sail around the whole world. But these people, these Chug-a-lugs, these Zakrezewskis, could never get to Mexico in a day. Even in a Sky Chief.

"What they do in that car?" Mary Kate asked Venita one evening as they sat on Mary Kate's front porch.

"They must fly," Venita said. "That car must be a rocket ship."

"No, they drive," Mikey said, a little pitcher. He was standing inside the screen door.

"Go to bed," his mother said.

Mikey went up to bed and wished he'd had a book to look up where Mexico was. He knew it was far. He remembered seeing it on a globe in school, but he couldn't remember where it was.

Cheryl had told him that they didn't just *go* to Mexico, they *were* Mexican.

"We speak Mexican too," Chris had said.

"Speak Mexican," Mikey demanded.

"I don't have to speak Mexican to prove it to you," Cheryl said.

"Ya'll ain't no Mexicans. Ya'll Polacks," Mikey said.

"No we aren't," Cheryl said. "And I'll speak Mexican to you just to show you. Adiós!" It came out "Ay-dee-oos." "That means goodbye, smarty. Look it up."

Mikey suspected she might be pulling his leg, but it made no difference. He had no way of looking up what "ay-dee-oos" was, and if Cheryl was lying, she would slip out of it. But Mikey liked this peachy, one-lipped pregnant girl.

Cheryl wasn't really lying. Her family did go to Mexico for a day every weekend. Mexico, New York, where they had lived. Jake drove, cruising down the thruway with the top down, doing seventy all the way. Angela sat next to him, an upper lip painted on for the trip. The kids sat in the back, the wind whipping through their hair. They had to lie down for most of the ride to keep from drowning in the stream of air.

When they came back on Saturday night, the car would be packed with beer and groceries, and Jake would have an attitude. He would be looped on Genesee. The children and Angela made trips back and forth to the car to unload it. Jake spent his time going over the car, letting up her top, shaking out her mats, ducking under her hood.

Arguing on the front porch was part of the ritual after the

return from Mexico. The radio would be cranked up, and the twangy music would begin bouncing off of the buildings. Things stayed pretty quiet until Jake had had his fifth or sixth quart. This was when the yelling began.

All summer Jake had been grumbling about their moving. It had been Angela's idea for them to live in All-Bright Court, to save money until they found a house. They had left Mexico so he could take a welding job at Capital. He had commuted for nearly a year, just he and his mistress out on the open road. Jake spent the week in Buffalo and drove home on weekends, but Angela couldn't see how they were saving money that way. So they all moved, and Angela found a job at a dye plant in Buffalo. She could see the money adding up.

It wasn't her fault they hadn't moved out of All-Bright Court. Jake was too lazy to look for a house. There were all kinds of houses for sale right in the neighborhood. They could *walk* and look at them.

He didn't want a house within walking distance of *this* place.

What did he expect, a house to come driving up looking for them?

No, what he did expect was some peace and quiet. And those kids. She couldn't control them, the twins. That was *her* job.

Didn't *he* think she worked? Didn't he ever think she might be tired?

From what? She didn't clean. The house was dirty.

She didn't care about *this* place. She wanted a house. *She* was saving money.

She was saving money, all right. She was starving him. Just look at him. He was wasting away.

He was skinny when she met him. How was that her fault? He was naturally skinny.

That was true, Jake was naturally skinny. In fact, he looked like a skinny Elvis. This did not endear him to the people of All-Bright Court.

Rumor had it that Elvis had said, "Ain't nothing a nigger can do for me 'cept buy my records and shine my shoes." No one knew when or where Elvis had said it, and if you asked anyone how he knew this, he would say, "Everybody know. Ain't no secret." If Jake had listened to Elvis instead of country and western, or if he had an upper lip to curl up at them, he might have been run out.

The arguments were enough to make people want to run him out. Every Saturday night, back and forth, back and forth, the family's dirty laundry waving in the wind, raggedy drawers, soiled bras, bloodstained sheets. They aired it all. Angela remained cool throughout these exchanges, but on the weekend after the Fourth, she lost it.

Jake was popping the top off his eighth quart when he started in on a different tack.

She was fucking around on him.

What? With who? She laughed.

That guy. She knew the one, the Italian guy at the factory. She knew the one.

There's tons of Italian guys at the factory.

She knew the one, the one that brought her home last week. Him?

Him! She was sick. *He* wouldn't come get her.

What did she expect? He was working on his car.

That figured.

She was changing the subject. Why was she fucking around on him? She knew how Italian men were, liking fat women.

He was crazy.

No he wasn't.

She knew Italians were animals, pigs.

His mother was Italian.

What was she trying to say about his mother? What was she trying to say about him?

He had said Italians were pigs. He could figure it out.

Then he jumped her. He rode her down off the porch and onto the front lawn, holding on to her like a rodeo rider who had grabbed hold of a steer too big for him to wrestle.

Angela shook him off and he rolled a few times. She ran to the porch, grabbed a beer bottle, and broke it against the building. Jake was too dazed and drunk to even stand up. Angela jumped on top of him. He fought her as hard as he could, all the while shouting for help.

But not one of the neighbors came. It was just the trash blowing up again, and besides, it was none of their business.

Angela slashed Jake's face with the bottle. The half-Indian ghost of a boy with the whole-Indian stupid drunk dead father saved Jake. He jumped on his mother's back, and though he wasn't strong enough to pull her off, his presence brought her back to her senses. She rolled off Jake and lay on the ground, weeping.

There were sirens coming, wailing closer and closer, and Jake's blood was dripping on the ground. Two white officers came on the scene, clubs drawn.

What a sight they saw. A skinny Caucasian man dripping blood all over, and he had pissed on himself. A nasty, bloody rag was pressed against his face. The cut was only a scratch, but a deep scratch, less than an inch from his left eye. He was crying, and she was crying, this pregnant white woman with a big smudge of orange lipstick on her chin.

Their kids were standing around them, wearing dirty underwear. Even in the darkness the stains on their drawers could be seen. A true mother's nightmare. The kids weren't crying. They looked stunned, and they were quiet, their hair standing up like oily feathers.

A crowd of Negroes, colored people, black people, had gathered. What were they calling themselves now? They were keeping their distance. Good. No trouble. Their eyes were glowing as they watched from the darkness.

No charges. No one wanted to press charges. But what was to be expected? *These* people living down here with *them*. What could you expect?

Things settled down after the fight. Jake and Angela were ashamed, and well they should have been. They had seen the way the cops had looked at them. They weren't *that* drunk. They could see that the cops were amused, giving each other sly looks from the corners of their eyes and smiling. Those bastards were smiling, and Jake knew, he just knew, they must have been Italians. Pigs. Treated them just like they were a bunch of niggers. They had to move.

Jake started taking the Star Chief out on weekdays. It hurt him to do it to her, to make her move. But after Angela came home, after she'd worked a ten-hour shift, taken two buses, cooked dinner, and washed the dishes, he and she would go sailing out of All-Bright Court. They never took the children.

It was on one of these nights that it happened: Mikey went into the Chug-a-lug house.

His mother had forbidden him from going into any of the children's houses. "You play outside. You don't know what people be doing in they houses. If I hear tell you been playing in somebody house, I'm a tear up your behind."

Mikey knew he was forbidden, and his mother's words were swimming around in his brain that evening.

He and some other children had been playing hide and seek out in the gloaming. This was the best time to play, when children could disappear into the shadows and slide around only half seen. Chris was it, and no one was to go off the row because the mothers would be calling them in soon. It did a child little good if he found the best hiding place a few rows over, if he sank into the deepest shadow, only to have his mother call him in before he could spring from it and win the game.

Chris was stationed at the side of the row, on the end by his house. He stood counting, and while the children scattered, he peeled paint from the building, and ate it.

"Let's hide together," Cheryl said to Mikey, "in my house. My parents aren't home."

"No," Mikey said. "Let's go hide at the other end of the row."

"What, are you afraid of going into a white person's house?"

"No." That was not it at all. He wanted to tell her that his mother did not allow . . . The right thing to say was swimming around in his brain, but it was drowning.

"I've been in colored people's houses. I've been in this boy Dennis's house. You know Dennis?"

"Yeah, but—"

"I don't believe you. I've never seen you with him. His mother won't let him come over this way."

"Who's not ready holler *I*," Chris yelled.

"*I!*" Mikey and Cheryl screamed together.

"Let's go in the back door. No one will see us," Cheryl said. "We'll win."

"We will win, but it seem like cheating," Mikey said.

"So?" Cheryl said. She led Mikey through the back door. Paulie was sitting right there in the window, but Mikey didn't even see him.

Not only was this the first time he was in someone's house without his mother's permission, it was a white person's house, a trashy white person's house. He wanted to look around, but Cheryl was pulling on his arm. She yanked him from the kitchen into the living room.

No lights were on on the first floor, and a blue light from outside filtered into the house. As Cheryl pulled on his arm, he felt both excited and scared. He was trying to see, but trying to avoid whatever dangers might come swooping out of the shadows. Unconsciously he began sniffing the air.

There was not one molecule of a familiar smell, no odor of boiled pork, black-eyed peas, no Dixie Peach. There was only a faint odor of yeasty sourness.

Cheryl led Mikey to the bottom of the staircase. He stopped cold.

"Come on. What's wrong with you? Scared?"

"No," Mikey said. He followed her upstairs and into a bedroom. She went to the window. While Cheryl looked out the window, Mikey stood by the door. There were two un-made beds. On one was a fat baby doll tangled in a sheet. There was a dresser with its top drawer missing. On top of the dresser was a lamp. No shade was on the lamp, and the naked bulb cast fat shadows in the room.

"We'll give Chris a few minutes. Then we'll sneak back out," Cheryl said.

Mikey wasn't listening.

Cheryl left the window and took her doll from the bed. "We're moving soon, to a real house, and I'm going to get a pony."

"You not going to move, and you not getting no pony," Mikey said.

"You're jealous," she said. "I am going to get a pony, and I'm going to name it Midnight if it's black. If it's white I'm going to call it Snowflake. If it's brown —" Cheryl dropped her doll. "Roach," she said, pointing at the wall. Mikey looked to where she was pointing. Over the dresser, a roach was crawling up the wall. Cheryl took off her sneaker and smashed it.

"You have roaches?" she asked.

"Yeah," Mikey said.

"That figures. My daddy says colored people bring roaches wherever they go. That's why we're leaving here. It's dirty," Cheryl said.

"Your daddy wrong. Colored folks don't bring roaches, and it ain't dirty here."

"Yes it is, and you know it. It's a slum," Cheryl said. She picked up her doll. "This is my baby."

The doll was naked. It was the kind of doll that had blinking eyes, and one was broken shut. The one shut eye and the doll's molded smile made it look as if she were winking. Mikey stared at the doll's one blue glass eye.

"Do you know where babies come from?" she asked.

"Yeah," Mikey said.

"Where, smarty?"

"I don't have to prove it to you by telling you," Mikey said. He could hear the game outside. Chris, the it, was catching children and calling them out. One, two, three.

"Where?" Cheryl pressed.

"I do know. They come from storks."

Cheryl laughed so hard her laughter filled the big, distorted shadows in the room. "That's a lie."

"My mama say —"

"That's a lie parents tell their kids so they won't have to tell them where babies *really* come from," Cheryl said.

Mikey walked over to where Cheryl was. She continued. "My mommy tried to tell me that one, but Daddy said, 'Don't lie to the kid. Tell her the truth.' Want me to show you how grown people get babies, or are you scared?"

Mikey could hear children screaming. They had been discovered and were trying to beat Chris back home.

Mikey looked at the doll on the floor. The other eye had blinked shut. "I'm not scared," he said.

Cheryl pulled down her shorts and underpants and reached to pull down Mikey's.

He was scared, so scared that for a few seconds he thought he had gone deaf. He let Cheryl pull down his pants and underpants, and he looked around the room as if he were being watched, as if his mother would materialize from one of the grotesque shadows. He could not see what any of this had to do with babies, and he had the feeling that this was a trick, that Cheryl would quickly pull on her clothes and run out and win the game.

Sound returned to the world. Right below the window there was squealing. Someone was making a dash for home, and Chris was shouting, "I got you. I got you."

Mikey stood still, waiting for Cheryl to make a run for it. He would beat her. He would pull up his clothes and be the first one out.

"Lay down with me on the bed," Cheryl said. She climbed onto her unmade bed. Mikey did not move. "Do you want to know or don't you?"

Mikey climbed onto the bed, his pants around his ankles.

"Lay on top of me."

Mikey stared at her. He did not think he heard her right. His heart was beating so hard that it was blocking his hearing again.

"Lay down on top of me. I'm not going to bite you."

Mikey heard Cheryl that time. "I'll squish you," he said.

"You won't squish me," she said, and pulled him down.

Mikey could feel himself sinking into her. He tried making himself lighter by holding his breath. Somehow, it seemed, by doing so he would stay afloat atop the softness, the moistness, the saltiness that was the sea of her body. He stiffened as he felt himself disappearing into her stomach, and he could not stop himself. Though there was something about this sinking, about this giving way, that he liked, he was frightened. It was as if her flesh were opening up and he were being drawn inside.

"You can get up," Cheryl said. "That's it."

Just as she spoke, the bedroom door opened. They both jumped up, their underpants and shorts twisted around their ankles. It was Paulie. He looked at them and, without saying a word, walked away.

They both pulled up their clothes, and as they went rumbling down the stairs, Mikey was thinking that there would be no explaining this to his mother. None. She was right: "You don't know what people be doing." And his father. Mikey knew he would be whipped, but that was the least of it. What would they think of him? Naked with a white girl, a trashy white girl, a Chug-a-lug.

Mothers were calling their children, and Chris was chanting, "Ollie ollie oxen free. Ollie ollie oxen free." The game was over.

At the landing at the bottom of the stairs Cheryl said, "We're home free." She could see that Mikey was not listening. "Paulie won't tell, O.K.? He won't. Come on, we can win. We're home free." She tried pulling him through the front door, but he broke free of her, busted out the back door, and headed for his house.

That night while he was in the tub, Mikey washed quickly. He did not want to give his mother or father a chance to come into the bathroom.

They did not come in, but Cheryl did. She came in through his mouth. A single hair of hers lay coiled at the back of his tongue. He had been scraping at it with his teeth, not knowing what it was until he pulled the yellow hair from his mouth.

He drew in a sharp breath, and he would have held it forever if he could, somehow thinking, hoping, wishing that by doing so he could keep his secret safe. If only he could stay there, holding it in, he could get lighter and lighter, light enough to float away.

But there was no need for Mikey to worry, for Paulie, like many children, could keep a secret better than an adult could. Besides, within the week they were gone, every last Chug-a-lug.

Jake and Angela had seen a house the first week they went out looking and had made an offer. Things began to move quickly, almost too quickly, the offer accepted, the loan approved. They left at night.

No one in All-Bright Court was sad to see them go. Mary Kate and Venita were sitting on the front porch, watching them pack up the Sky Chief. "I'm glad them trashy folks leaving," Mary Kate said.

"They probably skipping out on the rent," Venita said. "I don't know why they ever came here. Why would they come live 'round colored people?"

"I want to know who sold them nasty, trashy folks a house."

"I'm glad they going. Good riddance to bad news."

Mikey stood inside the front door, listening. "Mama?" he called.

"Boy, I thought you was watching TV with your daddy."

"He sleep, Mama. Mama, is we living in a slum?" he asked.

"Boy, you be coming up with some questions."

"Is this a slum?" he pressed.

His mother did not look at him. She cast her eyes into the night. "I suppose this is a slum. Why you ask that?"

"I just wanted to know." He sighed and went upstairs.

"That some boy," Venita said. "You got you a bright boy."

"I worry about him," Mary Kate said. "He keep things inside, brood over things."

"He going be all right," Venita said. "Where you think them folks moving?"

"I don't know," Mary Kate said. "I'm sure they moving to a nicer place than this."

Where the Zakrezewskis were moving was Niagara Falls, to a place Adam and Eve might envy. The Chug-a-lugs blew right out of All-Bright Court and landed in Love Canal.

13

WAKING UP

THERE WAS a war here last night. The people went into the streets and waged a war. They fought the buildings and cars and street lights. With rocks and sticks they raged against the night. They brought their anger and grief and pain out, and their shadows flew through the streets, black angels through the streets, given flight by a tempered-steel moon.

And from All-Bright Court wailing could be heard. It was coming through the walls, rising through the floorboards.

Mikey and his sisters sat on the stairs and watched their father cry. This was the first time they had seen him cry. He was not wailing, but they could hear wailing. It was coming through the walls. They could feel it under their feet.

Four hundred years of pain, four hundred years of sorrow, were being released. Their ancestors were waking up. They were standing inside the walls, and they were wailing from the other side. "How long, Lord? How long?" they were asking, and their sorrow shook the walls.

But their father was kneeling and sobbing into their mother's housedress. He was clinging to the dress and resting his head on their mother's pregnant stomach. Their mother was crying too, and she was moaning and rubbing their father's head with her small hands. Then the children began crying, though they did not know why. Martin Luther King had been killed, and it seemed all the world was crying. It was a time to cry. And Mikey and his sisters cried and clung to one another.

Their father was saying something. They could not hear what he was saying. Whatever it was, he was mumbling it into their mother's dress, whispering it into the baby's ear.

From the streets came the sound of the beating of angels' wings. The people were going to war. They were going up to Ridge Road. That is where the war took place, on the main street on the northern edge of town.

They raged against the night, turned over cars and burned them, attacked Ridge Road. They beat up on their own neighborhood. They beat up on themselves.

When the people returned to All-Bright Court, Mikey and his sisters and parents were standing on the porch. They were not crying anymore. They were shaking and watching the spoils being carried by. They saw televisions, and radios, and bottles of liquor, and cases of beer and pop, and bags of potatoes, and boxes of Fab, and bottles of Joy, and suits, and dresses, and roasts, and ten-pound buckets of chitterlings, and cartons of cigarettes being carried by. They saw Isaac and some other teenage boys skating by with their arms full of clothes.

"We broke into the rink too," Isaac said. "Go on up there and get ya'll some skates, kids. Go get anything ya'll want. We opened up all the stores. It's Christmas Day."

"Christmas," Mary said.

"There go Dennis," Mikey yelled.

"I'm going to get me something, Mike. Come on. I'm going to get me something. I'm going to get me something," Dennis sang.

"Can I go, Daddy?" Mikey asked.

"No, boy. You crazy? Them people stealing. Somebody going to get killed up there. Mark my word."

Dennis joined the rest of the crowd, and before it could go and come back again, flames could be seen rising to the north. Sirens could be heard, and the sound of breaking glass.

"They shooting," someone said. "It sound like shooting."

"Come on inside, ya'll," Mr. Taylor said. "When bullets come flying out a gun, they ain't got nobody's name on them." He saw his family inside and locked the door. He and his wife returned to the television, and they sent the children to bed. But they did not sleep.

Mikey went into his sisters' room. Dorene had her head under the blanket. "What you hiding from?" Mikey said.

Dorene said nothing until she heard the sound again. It was a helicopter flying overhead. "It's a war. It's just like on TV," Dorene said, and she began crying.

"Stop acting like a baby. You don't see Mary or Olivia crying. How can it be a war here?" Mikey asked.

"I don't know."

"Get out from under that blanket. It ain't no war. I'm telling you, see?"

"It's Christmas," Mary said.

"It's not no Christmas," Dorene said. "What is it, Mikey?"

"I don't know. It sound like a fight."

He crawled into bed with his sisters, and they listened to voices in the night. And when the voices were silenced, there was the wailing.

Their ancestors were waking up. They were standing inside the walls, and they were wailing from the other side.

Their sorrow shook the bedroom walls. Their sorrow lulled the children to sleep.

In the morning there was silence. The war was over. The wailing had stopped. Mr. Taylor was not going to work, and there was no school. He walked his family to Ridge Road. He wanted his children to see what had happened, and to remember this day. Mary was on his shoulders and Dorene clasped his hand. Mikey walked with his mother, and she pushed Olivia in a stroller.

On their way up Steelawanna Avenue, they saw a pack of dogs eating a roast the looters had dropped. There was broken glass everywhere. It sparkled in the morning sun.

"Pick me up, Daddy," Dorene begged.

"You too big for me to be picking up. Why you always want to be the baby? Just watch your step."

As the family made its way through the street, they saw mismatched shoes and skates scattered, a new radio smashed, dresses and pants trampled, skeletons of cars still smoking.

"This a shame," Mrs. Taylor said. "Just a excuse to steal. If he was alive, he would be sick."

"If who was alive?" Dorene asked.

"Dr. King," her father said. "He not even cold yet, and see what we done."

As they approached Ridge Road, they could see the damage. The A & P, the cleaners, the Jubilee Theatre, the roller rink, the laundry, the five-and-dime, the drugstore, the barbershop, and even Dulski's — all looted and burned. Only the churches had been spared.

At the corner of Steelawanna and Ridge Road there were white soldiers in green, carrying rifles. They formed a wall blocking the street, standing shoulder to shoulder, protecting spoiled meats, singed clothes, charred buildings.

The northern sections of the plant could be clearly seen

through the remains of the buildings. "Damn," Mr. Taylor said. "You can see all the way to the coke ovens." He pointed. "That's where I work, kids." Mary and Dorene and Olivia looked, but Mikey didn't. He wasn't interested.

Before the wall of soldiers a small crowd had gathered, a crowd that was sullen and angry. Their faces were ashen masks carved by sorrow. And from the collection of dun masks there rose a tired voice.

"They killed him."

"Who, Daddy?" Dorene asked from behind her father's pant leg.

"Martin Luther King, stupid. Daddy already told you that," Mikey said.

"Ya'll ain't heard the news?" a voice asked. "It was on the radio this morning."

A mask separated itself from the crowd, and behind it was a tall and thin yellow man. He walked over to Mr. Taylor and whispered in his ear.

Mr. Taylor put Mary down and took his wife by the hand. "Mikey, you stay here with the girls. Don't ya'll move." He and his wife walked closer to the wall and looked over it.

"There he is," the man said. "See him there."

A small figure flanked by wings of dried blood was lying in front of the A & P. Next to the blanketed form was a canned ham, and a mounted policeman was standing guard.

"That's Dennis. They ain't say his name on the radio 'cause they ain't found his mama yet. He was hit by a stray 'fore them guards or cops even showed up last night. I'm telling you, it's a shame. They left his body laying there all night."

Mikey and Mary played in the grass while Dorene sat on a curb next to the stroller and peeked through the legs of the wall, not wanting to look, not wanting to see, but there was something moving on the other side, back and forth, back and forth, there were things moving, and before she realized it, she was staring at the face of a white man that had drifted down below the wall, a face she recognized from television, a newsman, whose face passed in and out of her sight quickly, but Dorene knew why it was here.

"Come on now, Kate. I told you, you can't change the world," Mr. Taylor said, and Dorene looked up to see her parents standing over her. Her mother was crying and her father's arm was around her mother's shoulders. Mikey and Mary gathered around them.

"Get on up from there, girl. Let's go."

Dorene jumped from the curb and followed her parents. She and Mikey walked together, and their father had put Mary in the stroller with Olivia.

"Ain't no telling where his mama is."

"Who mama?" Mikey asked.

"Maybe some good will come of this," Mr. Taylor said.

"Who mama?" Mikey asked.

"Shut up," Dorene said. "You so stupid."

14

JESÚS

JESÚS WAS a black man with nappy hair. Around his eyes there was a hint of something. Around his tiny black eyes, somewhere in the curve of his brow, were the lies of white men. Inside his eyes, lost somewhere in the well of their blackness, were the promises made to an Indian woman. All the blacks called him *Jesus*, just like it was meant to be.

They could not figure out Puerto Ricans anyway. They didn't know what category to put them in. They were not quite black and not quite white, but exactly what they were was not clear. But Jesús ruined things. It was clear that he was black, even if around his eyes there were whispers of other worlds. Around many of the blacks' eyes the same thing whispered.

You could knock on almost any door in All-Bright Court and find someone to repeat it. "Yeah, my grandma was a Crow." "My great-grandaddy was Cherokee." True or not, it was something to brag on, a place to locate the wave in someone's hair, a place that held the origin of the blush of redness in one's skin, a place to touch the hardness and high-ness of a cheekbone. Even if it was a white man they saw in the flame of their faces, even if it was the whisper of a lie some white man had breathed into their grandmother's breasts, still caught up in the tangles of their hair, it was easier to believe they were seeing an Indian. It was exotic, untraceable, a way of putting down roots, of pushing their toes right through the slabs of stone under their feet and staking claim to an entire continent. They were the doubly dispossessed.

But the Puerto Ricans could also lay claim to disposses-sion. Their wealth amounted to no more than a handful of dried beans. If their lives had meant more to white men, if the copper in their skin could have been spun into gold, they would not have been living in All-Bright Court.

Jesús's family was like the other families coming from Puerto Rico, only he was different. He was nothing like his brother César or his sister Gloria or his parents.

Mrs. Taylor had said to her neighbor Billie Hines, "Maybe Jesús the milkman son."

"Naw. They ain't got no coloreds down there. You seen any of them that was colored?" Billie asked.

"No," Mrs. Taylor said. "But girl, they some good-looking people, got that pretty hair and smooth skin. There more and more of them. Every time you turn around, an-other bunch of them moving in."

Billie said, "I tell you this. I don't like them. How can you stand a whole family living in back of you?"

"They don't bother nobody. Isaac be over there in that house."

"That figure, though, that he would be with them. Them people stink. They loud and nasty, they do nothing but bring roaches. And they taking away jobs in the plant, jobs from our men," Billie said.

"They just trying to live," Mrs. Taylor said.

"And the names they give they kids. There a girl in my child class name Con*cep*tion, and look at them boys behind you, *Je*sus and Caesar. What the hell kind of names them?"

Mrs. Taylor said, "Yeah, it seem like they would know that Jesus and Caesar was enemies."

"That boy so black because God done cursed him for his mama throwing *His* child name on him."

When Jesús's family had moved in, they had two skinny chickens that walked around in a small circle of wire. Sometimes, when it was quiet late at night, Mikey would wake up because he was too hot, or too cold, or he needed a drink of water, and he would hear the chickens out there, the beating of their wings. He would get up and watch them pecking at each other and rising in the air.

But before anyone could call the rent office about the chickens, they disappeared. It was said that Greene took them. "It must of been her," it was said. "There was a full moon last night."

Isaac and his friend Rick could be seen passing through this dusty yard where the chickens once were. Isaac had met César during Isaac's last year in O.E. When César came home from school, Rick and Isaac would go over to his house and sit in the living room. They drank Iroquois beer and waited for Gloria to walk through on her way to get ice water, or on her way to the store, or on her way to nowhere, just walking through, her pants a second skin, her short hair a raven's wings. She was always on her way to somewhere else, but she had winked at Rick. For months she had been in flight, and someday she would land. Rick wanted to fly away with her, to be a blackbird flying over All-Bright Court. He was leaving anyway. He had joined the army.

"I'm going before they come for me. I got the feeling my number coming up. You lucky you went to O.E.," Rick said to Isaac. "You lucky too, Caesar. Uncle Sam don't bother with O.E. people."

"I don't want to go noway," Isaac said. "Them gooks ain't playing games. Look at Halloween. Looking at him some scary shit. Let them gooks and white boys fight the Commies. If they come over here, I'll get my daddy's piece and ice a few. You should go to Canada, Rick. Shit, you could walk there from here."

"I would fight," César said. "Go to war for me country."

"This ain't none of your goddamn country," Rick said. "You crazy if you think this your country. White people care less about ya'll than they do about us."

"This is me country, but I would no fight for white people. I would fight for democracy," César said.

"Fuck democracy," Rick said. "I'm going in Uncle Sam's army 'cause I ain't got nowhere else to go. And what's a nigger going to do in Canada?"

"Same thing a nigger do here," Isaac said. "Go on up there and get a job in a plant. They got steel plants up there too."

"We live across the street from a steel plant here. That don't mean I got a job," Rick said. "I been laid off almost a year. I'm telling you, Canada for white boys. You got to have money, know somebody, blend in. I ain't got no money, don't know nobody, and where a nigger going to hide in Canada?"

The one thing Rick had to look forward to was Gloria. He kept hoping she would stop and wink at him again, and one day she did stop. She called to him from the kitchen. "Ricky," she said. "*Ven acá.*"

Rick did not move.

"*¡Mira!* Come here. *Ven acá.*"

The beer lifted him from the sofa and carried him into the kitchen.

"Dance with me," Gloria said, and she grabbed his two hands, big and useless, and held them in hers.

He danced an awkward salsa with her, to a song playing on the radio. To him the beat was foreign.

"*Tú bailas bien,*" Gloria said, and Rick smiled. In the sallowness of the kitchen, the pace of his life changed. As Gloria began to cha-cha, Rick could not keep up with her, and she let go of his hands.

Her feet moved faster. One, two, one two three. One two one two three. Onetwoonetwothree. Onetwoonetwothree-onetwoonetwothree. Gloria spun around the chairs as if they were couples on a dance floor, and when she flashed around the table Rick saw her, just for an instant, rise off the linoleum and fly toward him.

He reached for her, reached out for dear life, and he grabbed her by the waist as his lips sought the heat of her neck.

It was just then that Jesús appeared at the back door and leaned on the doorjamb. The wells of his eyes were bottomless. He began spitting out words in Spanish, and so did Gloria, and around Rick's head spun a room of o's and a's, spinning and singing like big and angry tops.

César jumped up as Jesús was pushing Gloria toward the living room, but before he could get there, Rick had jumped on Jesús's back and had ridden him to the floor. That was all Rick could do. Jesús flipped him over his head and dragged him into the back yard. Gloria, César, and Isaac ran out after them.

"*Peleá,*" Jesús yelled, and he circled Rick, his two fists knotty rocks.

"*¡Levantate!*" Jesús said, and a crowd was beginning to form. The less brave stood on their porches, inside their back doors, or peeked from behind curtains.

Mikey watched from his back door, eating a Fluffernutter

on Wonder bread, but when the braver spectators came and made themselves a circle, he ran upstairs and watched from his bedroom window.

The crowd closed the circle in the yard at 50 All-Bright Court, leaving only Rick and Jesús in the center, and the only way Rick could get out was to fight.

Rick stood up. He began circling, looking for a way out, for a way to drop Jesús and just get away, but his head was humming from the beer. While he listened to the hum, Jesús dropped him with a right.

"Get 'em. Get 'em," Mikey said, jumping up and down. He dropped his sandwich and began throwing punches before the window.

Rick lay on the ground, blood dripping from his nose.

"*¡Levantate!*" Jesús taunted.

"*¡Basta!*" Gloria screamed. "*¡Basta, Jesús!*"

"Did you hear that?" someone said. "She calling her brother a bastard. Did you hear that? She calling her brother a bastard in the yard."

"I always thought he was," someone else whispered.

"That's a shame, telling all they business in the street. But you know them people."

Rick did not get up, and Jesús strutted around him, kicking his feet through the dirt and puffing out his chest. "*Negro,*" he spat at Rick, and he grabbed Gloria by the arm and pulled her into the house. The crowd parted before him. In a moment only César and Isaac remained in the clearing yard.

César was left to explain Jesús, to pull some reasons out of the cloud of dust he had kicked up. But it was hard to find even one. Whatever reason there was seemed to be dissipating, settling back down in the earth, and as César knelt over Rick, all he could say was, "He alway want to be the boss. He don't boss nobody. Don't pay no attention to him."

Jesús's actions only helped confirm what people suspected. He was not his father's son. He was not the son of the man who spoke English, broken and hard like pieces of brick, a man who, like Gloria, and César too, had the hair of a raven, a man who had a gold tooth in the front of his mouth, a man who sold shaved ice from his back door in summer, and in the winter sold "*ron o vino*" from under the counter of his cousin's store, a man who held the breasts of the blackest of women in his eyes. Jesús was not the son of the man who had been seen leaving Greene's house singing Spanish songs to the night winds.

Jesús surrounded himself with every Puerto Rican he could find, and spoke Spanish loudly. Rick was the first black person Jesús had ever talked to, and he used his words as weapons, sprayed Spanish into Rick's face, shot it into his back. Jesús made it clear he was not one of them.

That night Rick and Isaac stood in front of the Red Store pitching pennies under a street lamp. It was after nine, and the store was closed. The warmth that had been held in its bricks was gone.

The wind, the Hawk from the lakefront, was blowing. Somehow it managed to get by the plant, to climb around the monster. Once the sun went down, the Hawk seemed to seek out the land, to come looking for something it had lost, something that it could never find in the darkness. Instead, it punished all it found there. It swooped and rose and turned corners on a wing.

As Rick and Isaac stood there in the night wind, it cut them to the bone. Isaac said, "Let's split, Rick. It's cold as hell out here."

"You just saying that 'cause you losing. I ain't going in. I'm waiting for Jesús," Rick said.

"Forget about it, man. Caesar cool. He hip."

"I'm not talking about Caesar. I'm talking about his brother. The nappy-head Puerto Rican bean-eating crazy-ass black nigger. Who he think he is? Calling me a Negro. Who *he* think he is?"

Isaac did not know what to say. He looked into Rick's eyes, searching for what he should say. "I don't know who he thinks he is."

"I'll tell you who he is. He ain't nothing. He ain't shit. I'm going to show him that. I saw him heading up Ridge Road way earlier. He be back. He got to come back," Rick said.

"You going to basic next week. Let it slide," Isaac said.

"No. He ain't have to act that way. It was just a dance."

"Well, you better jump him. That's all I'm saying. Jump his ass—and carry something. You know he packing. You want me to get you something?"

"Don't worry about that. I got me a blade. I'll use it if I have to."

"It's cold," Isaac said. Rick did not respond. "It's going to be plenty hot where you going. You going be wishing you had some of this cold. They say it get to be two hundred degrees over there."

Rick cut his eyes at Isaac. "Sometimes I know why they sent you to O.E. What kind of stupid shit is that? Two hundred degrees."

Isaac bent down and began picking up the pennies from the game. He did not want to look at Rick. He was looking at the ground when he said, "That's just what I heard."

"And you'll never know," Rick said. Isaac looked at him, looked into his eyes for what he should say, but he could find nothing.

It was not until after eleven that Jesús appeared. Rick saw him walking down Steelawanna, his head bowed against the wind, his hands in his pockets. "I think that's him," Isaac said.

"I see him," Rick said.

"I got your back," Isaac said.

Rick and Isaac stood against the cold wall, hidden in the enormous shadow the store cast. Invisible and formless and black. They let Jesús pass them, let him get a big lead before they struck out after him. He was already halfway across the field when they caught sight of him again. They were slowed because they went single file down the path, trying not to rustle the dried weeds. Rick led the way, and Isaac walked quickly behind him, shaking.

Rick caught up to Jesús as he reached his block. Rick had the chance to turn back, and he almost did when he saw the yard at 50, but he moved on. He ran up behind Jesús, closed his arms around his neck, and rode him to the ground.

Upstairs in his bed, Mikey awoke. He was cold, too cold to get up and close his window. He heard a sound coming from outside, like the beating of wings. He left his bed and went to the window despite the cold. He saw two figures on the ground right in his back yard, rolling in the grass, and there was a third figure standing in the shadow, or was it a shadow? Mikey seemed to be the only witness to the fight, and he would have a story to tell. He stood quietly, punching the air, urging them on. "Get 'em, get 'em," he whispered, wishing he could see better, wishing he could hear. But there was nothing to hear except the beating of wings, until someone shouted, "Isaac." The suddenness of the sound scared Mikey. It echoed off the buildings, and there it was again, "Isaac." Mikey looked for Isaac, looked toward the shadow, but the shadow was gone. He stopped cheering and shrunk down, peeking over the window sill.

Squares of yellow appeared. And then a rectangle of light,

long and wide, opened up in the blackness of the yard. César came out of it. Mikey could see Jesús there on top of someone, sitting on someone's chest, and he could see the blade of a knife arching through the air. Mikey heard screaming, but it wasn't the voice that had called for Isaac. César pulled his brother off of the figure on the ground. César was yelling, and as he and Jesús ran toward their house, they set tops spinning through the air. Their words spun and spun and ran off into the night.

Mikey could see the man on the ground was Rick. There was blood on his neck, on his hands, on his jacket. He was still, lying on his back as though he were looking up at the sky, counting the stars. The rectangle closed over him.

Mikey ran to his bed. He closed his eyes and pulled the covers over his head. He could hear screaming. Doors were opening, and there was more screaming, and voices below, under his window. He heard his parents get up, first his father, then his mother. They ran downstairs and the back door opened. His mother shrieked. The door closed. There were sirens. His parents' footsteps were on the stairs.

Sleep, sleep, sleep, he thought. Be sleep. He turned his head to the wall. The footsteps entered his room and the light came on. He held his breath.

"He sleep," his mother said. Her voice was shaky. His window was closed. "He lucky. Kids can sleep through anything."

His father said, "No point in no ambulance coming. That boy dead."

"I want to leave here. We got to move," his mother said. She was crying.

"Move? To where? White people want us right here," his father said.

Mikey held his breath. His heart hurt like he had been

running in some great race. His mother was crying. The light went out and the door closed. The footsteps left. Mikey breathed out.

Be sleep. Be sleep.

In the morning Mikey awoke, surprised to find he had even slept. He could hear his father up, walking around, getting dressed for work. Martin, the new baby, was crying, and his mother was moving through the kitchen below. He was afraid to lift his head from under the covers, afraid to get up and look out the window. He thought he would see Rick there.

But Rick was gone. He was gone like he had never been there. And Jesús was gone too. He had flown away.

15

FAST TRACK

THE PEOPLE of All-Bright Court expected to see new stores rise from the ashes of Ridge Road, as if rain and sun would start a new cycle, buildings would come pushing through the blackness, incipient and translucent shafts of green. They had the notion they were part of the civilized world. Surely no one could expect them to live in a war zone. But the people came to know they were living in another world, a dying planet that was spinning away from what they had come to know. They had pulled civilization down around them.

Not one of the burned buildings was reopened. The charred remains were left as they were, a testament. Over on the other side of the bridge in Capital Heights, the world kept right on spinning, full of life and services. Life continued, even in their dying world.

Men filed in and out of the plant. Clouds of orange scudded overhead. Silver fell from the sky. Beneath the roar of the stacks, parents went about figuring out how to raise their children among the ruins. In every city that had gone up in flames, in every other project and run-down house, black and brown parents were trying to figure out the same thing. What they wanted was a way out, if not for them, then at least for their children. At the end of the summer when a man walked on the moon, a chance came for Mikey.

The previous spring he had taken an achievement test and had done well, well enough to be considered "gifted."

Mikey nearly missed taking the test. He had a cold and a slight fever on the day of the test, but his mother sent him anyway. She had received a note from his teacher, Mrs. Brezenski, stating that there would be a morning of testing. All of the children had to attend.

With ringing ears, a headache, and a dripping nose, Mikey had sat and answered the questions. He held his head in one hand and wrote with the other. He carefully filled in the ovals with his number 2 pencil, wiping his nose with his father's big, soft handkerchief. It was completely wet after the first half hour. All Mikey wanted to do was go home. His mother had promised he could stay home for the afternoon when he came back for lunch. She would make him tea with honey, and instead of watching her soap operas, she would let him watch cartoons. He finished the test and went home and slept the afternoon away on the couch. Neither he nor his parents thought more of the matter.

Mikey and his classmates had taken tests like these before, filled in ovals or rectangles with number 2 pencils issued by their teachers. The only students who ever heard any results were the ones who were pronounced "slow" or "problem learners." Their parents would receive a letter from the school requesting a meeting. There the parents would be assaulted with numbers that told them why their child had to go to the O.E. school. Even Puerto Rican parents, some of whom could grasp only a few words of what they were being told, patiently nodded their heads, acquiescing to the truth. Numbers typed neatly on clean white paper told a truth so absolute they dared not question it. Quietly, year by year, students vanished. Though the slow and the problem learners were identified, no one noticed the aberrations at the other end of the scale. Just as the slow were conjured out of the numbers, so were the gifted. But their names were locked in a gray file cabinet in the principal's office.

After the urban wars their names were released. The country was filled with anger, guilt, fear. These feelings, just as much as a true sense of altruism, led to the formation of groups like D.O.V.E.

D.O.V.E. was a nonprofit organization formed in Chicago to help inner-city students—those students Deserving Of a Viable Education. It was the organization's mission to find gifted inner-city students and place them in the best schools, the best being the New England prep schools. Exeter, Andover, Milton, Concord, Groton. D.O.V.E. placed younger children, those not old enough to board, in schools near them. Mikey's name came to the organization through Mrs. Brezenski.

She had not told Mikey's parents she had sent his name in, because she did not want to raise their hopes. D.O.V.E. had his name released from the file cabinet, but no one contacted Mrs. Brezenski until the week before school was to start in the fall. A place had been found for Mikey in a private school.

Mrs. Brezenski called his parents to the school. "Your son did very well on the achievements we gave last spring. He did so well, in fact," she said, handing a brochure to Mrs. Taylor, "that these people have procured a scholarship for him to a private school in Buffalo. Classes have not begun yet. The admissions officer says he can start this year. Next week."

Mrs. Taylor held the glossy brochure. On the cover was a picture of a lone black boy surrounded by a group of white boys. All of them were laughing.

Mrs. Brezenski explained the organization while the Taylors tried to read the information they had been presented. "You see, they are concerned with giving children a viable education, 'viable' being the operative word. The acronym is not just clever, but apropos. Your son has the chance to be a little ambassador, a dove of peace who can teach so much to the other boys at Essex."

"What school?" Mr. Taylor asked.

"Oh, I'm sorry," Mrs. Brezenski said, handing them a catalog. "The Essex Academy is one of the finest prep schools in western New York. I'm going to be honest with you. Michael is a very bright boy. I don't have to tell you that. There's not much we can do for a boy like him in a ghetto school. He's gifted, and he deserves a chance to have a quality education. If you let him go to Essex, he will give the boys there a chance to learn that Negroes are real people, just like white people. A boy like Michael can help change the future, help bring about a truly colorblind society, and he will receive a fine education, one of the best educations money can buy. He's been accepted to a wonderful school, and he can go for free."

"Things seem kind of rushed," Mr. Taylor said. "When we got to let you know?"

"As soon as possible. Tomorrow would be great. I'm sorry about the haste, but this slot opened up suddenly when a boy from Niagara Falls canceled out," Mrs. Brezenski said. "Think it over. This is the chance of a lifetime."

Mikey's parents discussed it that night when the children were in bed.

"Sam, I want him to have a good education, but he too young to go all the way to Buffalo to school."

Samuel said, "I think he need a good education too. Do you see him getting one out here?"

"I don't know. He getting more of a education than we got at his age."

"What's that saying? Segregated schools, not enough books, not enough nothing. We ain't had nothing."

"I know you right," Mary Kate said. "But Sam, he just a little boy, and we fenna send him to a school full of white people, and that teacher, the way she was carrying on. He going to be a dove. Look at this little book the teacher give us. How many coloreds you see? What's going to happen to my baby all alone?"

"Come on, Kate. He ain't no baby. I think that teacher was just saying they got the best there. We want the best for him. Maybe he can teach them white boys something. It's probably *some* Negro boys there. They just didn't put them in the book. He be all right. And I think he can handle it. He a smart boy. You heard what his teacher said. The boy got a gift. We got to give him a chance. We never had no chance. It ain't going to cost us nothing. How can we hold him back? If he not happy, we can always take him out."

They agreed to let Mikey go after they toured the campus. Samuel took the next day off from work. Mary Kate had Venita come over and sit with the children while she, Samuel, and Mikey went. All three were impressed by what they saw.

The fifty-acre campus was tucked in the northwest corner of Buffalo. The gray stone, slate-roofed buildings were surrounded by well-groomed lawns, perfectly cut hedges. There was a football field, lacrosse field, baseball field, a field house, a swimming pool, tennis courts, squash courts. The splendor they saw was blinding. They had entered a different world. Their guide was a white boy dressed in a blue blazer, khaki pants, a white shirt, blue-and-gray-striped tie. They didn't ask any questions.

Essex arranged for Mikey's transportation. Mrs. Cox would take him until he learned how to catch the bus. Mrs. Cox was a cafeteria worker at Essex who lived in Lackawanna, not that far from All-Bright Court, in one of the old houses on School Street.

On the first morning Mikey was to go to Essex, he put on his uniform and stood before his mother for inspection. She decided his neck looked dirty. She was out of alcohol, so she scrubbed his neck with Clorox.

"My neck clean," Mikey said.

"It don't look too clean to me," his mother said, "and you wearing that white shirt. I can't have you going off to that school having white people thinking you nasty. They not going to think it's just you nasty. They going to think all black boys is nasty. They think that anyway, that we nasty."

"How you know what white people think, Mama? You don't know no white people," Mikey said.

"Don't you give me no back talk, boy. You go to that school and mind your manners. Hear me? Don't go there asking a whole bunch of questions."

"I won't, Mama. I'm going to be good, and I'm going to make friends. You'll see."

"I'm not sending you to this school to make friends. I'm sending you to learn. Your friends right here in this house, hear me?" his mother said.

His sisters laughed. Their mother had descended on them before with a bottle of alcohol and a rough cloth. She had attacked their knees and elbows, their necks, their feet. She tried to scrub some of the blackness from their small bodies.

"Why your knees so black? I don't believe they that black. Go get me the alcohol and a washrag," she would say. And she would scrub her children until they were raw, but very seldom would she find any dirt on them.

"I guess your knees really that black," she would say if she found no dirt. If she found dirt, she would say, "See here, you nasty," and she would show them the cloth to prove it.

This morning his sisters watched Mikey squirm, and so did his baby brother, Martin. The baby took the cue from his sisters and laughed when they laughed.

"Ya'll don't be laughing at me," Mikey said.

"Don't ya'll be laughing," their mother said. "I'll get ya'll next."

There was no dirt on Mikey's neck. "I guess your neck really that black," their mother said.

"Now I smell like bleach, Mama," Mikey said. He wanted to cry because his neck was burning. And there was a horn blowing outside, Mrs. Cox.

Mikey's mother wiped off his neck with a wet cloth. She kept wiping and sniffing until the smell was gone. "Now let me take a look at you," she said. She sucked her teeth. "Dorene, run upstairs and get the Vaseline."

"What's wrong, Mama?" Mikey said.

"What's wrong? What's wrong? You look like a ash cat. You ain't put no grease on your face and hands. You can't leave out of here like this. What them white people going to think?"

Dorene came down with the grease, and there was a knock on the front door. Dorene let Mrs. Cox in.

She was a thin woman dressed in a white uniform. She smiled as she entered the house. "Is your mother in?"

"Good morning," their mother said, entering the living room, wiping her hands on a towel. "We running a little late, ma'am."

"Call me Sue. And your name is Mary, right?"

"Yes ma'am, Mary Kate."

"She said call her Sue," Mary said.

"Hush your mouth," their mother said. "Wasn't nobody talking to you. You speak when somebody speaking to you."

"These are all your children?"

"Yes. This is Mary, Dorene, Olivia, Martin, and you met Michael. He ready," their mother said, wiping a thin film of Vaseline on his face and hands until they shone like a polished cherry.

"What a beautiful family, and another on the way. When is the baby due?"

"After the first of the year . . . Ya'll better be going."

"Yes, you're right, Mary Kate. We wouldn't want him to be late his first day," Mrs. Cox said, catching hold of Mikey's hand.

"Now, you be a good boy," their mother said as Mikey and Mrs. Cox left the house. "You do your best and you be all right." She thought she was going to cry, but she held it in. He looked so smart in his blue blazer, his khaki pants, his blue-and-gray-striped tie. He was a gift.

As he came to the end of the sidewalk, he turned Mrs. Cox's hand loose and ran back to his mother. He hugged her, and she bent and kissed him.

"I'm going to try, Mama," he said. And then he was off and running.

16

EBB

BLITZKRIEG. That is what it seemed like to the men of Capital. Industrywide, one hundred thousand steelworkers were losing their jobs. That many men being displaced did not seem to be a random strike of lightning. The loss seemed deliberate, planned and executed to catch them unawares. Blitzkrieg.

In the last week of July in 1972, the news hit the papers. Many of the men were out on the road on their proletariat vacations, supporting their brothers in the U.A.W. by piloting American-made land yachts across the country, cruising to the Jersey shore, Ripley's Believe It or Not Museum, Old Faithful, South of the Border, Niagara Falls. On these journeys, the wives collected brown glass mugs with clumsy wooden handles, ceramic toothpick holders, and salt and pepper shakers, all imprinted with the names of the places they visited.

The men had not even struck when the contract had run out. In good faith, they blindly entered an area as vast as the mid-Atlantic: binding arbitration. The contract was going to expire just before the beginning of the school year. With binding arbitration, their children would be sure to have clothes, shoes, milk and lunch money. The rent or mortgage could be paid. Those workers who wanted to could even take vacations. Their demands were few. They wanted cost-of-living increases for the length of the three-year contract, something they had not had since their 1956 contract. They wanted production to stop for two weeks in the summer so they could all be out of the plants during the hottest weather. The rank and file also wanted to make it clear that it did not support the most ludicrous proposal anyone had ever come up with — that the steelworkers should give up the right to strike.

There were rumors that management was going to try to write a no-strike clause into the new contract. The men never had any right to walk out except when a contract expired. This new proposal would take away the right altogether, except for strikes called over local grievances. There would never be a chance the men could strike on a national level. Though none of the men liked to strike, the very suggestion that the right should be eliminated was outrageous.

Samuel had heard it. It sounded crazy to him. He had told Mary Kate, "I don't like it, but that union president, Petrovich, got his stupid ideas. I don't understand him. He used to work in the mills."

"Ya'll the ones keep voting him in. This the third time."

"It ain't no 'ya'll.' I ain't vote for him."

"You ain't voted at all, pay all them dues, for what? You don't even keep up with nothing they doing in that union," Mary Kate said.

"All I know is, there ain't going to be no need for no union 'cause there ain't going to be no plant."

"Don't say that, Samuel."

"It's the truth. They going to keep taking and taking till the next thing you know we going to be paying to work there. Let me tell you something. The union always hold the threat of a strike over management head to keep the companies honest. Neither side want a strike. It sure ain't a thing I ever wanted, but it's the only chip we got to throw on the table. Take that chip away, and there go the game, hear me?"

The men worked for three months while waiting for the 1971 contract to come through. The agreement they reached with management did not give the men much. They received cost-of-living increases, but they were given twenty cents an hour the first year, and eleven cents the next two years. The no-strike clause was not in the contract.

Eight months lapsed between that agreement and the headline in the *Buffalo Star*: MASSIVE LAYOFFS IN STEEL. The caption over the lead story was, "Capital to lay off 2,500."

Samuel was in the second week of his vacation when the news came. He had spent the time at home because he did not feel well enough to take his family anywhere. In the winter he had developed a chronic cough that a company doctor diagnosed as bronchitis. But Samuel had kept on working, breathing in coal dust, facing the Hawk on the lakefront, the heat of the coke ovens. By spring the cough was worse, but he never went back to the doctor. He worked right into the summer, worked himself into pneumonia. His first week of vacation he slept, Mary Kate shushing the children, chasing them from upstairs, making them tiptoe around. When the news came the second week, Samuel got out of bed.

He went to a meeting called at the union hall. "That lame duck Petrovich has sold us out!" a red-faced man yelled at the crowd of men. Samuel tuned the man out. He did not come to hear a speech. All he wanted to know was if he was going to have a job.

The news he was able to get he passed on to Mary Kate. "They going to be sending out letters right away, by the end of the week."

"That quick?"

"Yeah, that quick. What's the point in waiting? I wish they could have just told us today, face to face. It's cowardly, waiting till so many men on vacation to announce the lay-offs. I bet they knew about it before the contract came in."

"It ain't just Capital, Sam. It's everywhere. You read the paper. One hundred thousand men," Mary Kate said. "You think somebody sat back someplace and waited till now to tell ya'll?"

"Hell, yeah. You think management was going to say anything like this at contract time? If they know it now, they knew it then. That's what that binding-arbitration jazz was all about, getting us to work while they got that new contract."

"They say this at that meeting?" Mary Kate asked.

"Something like that. I wasn't half paying attention, but I ain't no fool. You really think somebody sat down last week and decided all this?"

"I don't know. They not going to lay you off, is they? You been there too long," Mary Kate said.

"I'll tell you this, they ain't doing it just on seniority. I don't think I'm going to be laid off."

The men waited for the letters. Black and white, young and old, they were thrown into a lottery. Men who had worked five, ten, twenty years, those who had suffered burns, broken limbs, who had chronic bronchitis, emphysema, asbestos poisoning, black lung, all waited and hoped they would not be turned out.

Capital was "scaling down," "cutting production." Temporarily. No man wanted to believe he would be laid off. Even if he was, he would be called back. The truth was that Capital was firing 2,500 men. In order to compete with foreign steel companies, Capital had to cut back on the cheapest part of the machinery.

Germany had become prosperous again. It did not seem the Germans could rise from the broken brick of a nation, from the split will of a people. They did not want war, these new Germans of the West. The West Germans were allies, not enemies. The Japanese were no longer enemies either. Along with the West Germans, they were exporting steel made more cheaply in modern plants, plants built after World War II. With aid from the United States, from companies like Capital, Japan and West Germany had been able to climb aboard the capitalist juggernaut. Now, just twenty-seven years after the war, they were threatening to take over the controls.

The men did not talk about it among themselves. The women did.

"Is Moses worried?" Mary Kate asked Venita, looking off into the night as they sat together on the Taylors' porch.

"Yeah, girl. He act like he ain't. He say he ain't going to be laid off."

"Samuel the same way, say the same thing," Mary Kate said.

"They both started there 'bout the same time. If one get let go, the other probably will too."

By the end of the week no letter had come for Moses or Samuel. The lottery had spared them. It was a matter of luck, of a hawk swooping through their lives, of not being plucked up, not this time. Like all the men who had been spared, they felt guilty. But it was not guilt that caused them to cast their eyes away from their brothers. Their gratefulness, sanguine and sensual, as raw as the passion a man can feel for another man's wife, caused them to look elsewhere, shamed them into silence.

For those who had not been spared — Jesús's father, Billie Hines's husband, and even Jake Zakrezewski, the patriarch of the Chug-a-lug clan — there was anger.

But a man whose anger is white-hot enough to consume the world can be made to stand in line by the church and the state so long — for food baskets, food stamps, used clothing, fuel assistance, unemployment checks, welfare checks, recertification — that his anger can be reduced to a single candlepower. His rage can become a sallow wavering flame, barely capable of illuminating the contents of an egg, and susceptible to the slightest wind.

17

DELIVERING

STANDING in the kitchen, Mikey was washing a bar of Ivory soap. He turned the fat cake over and over in his hands and watched as the blackness dripped from it, forming gray clouds in the sink.

"Your hands look like your daddy's" was what his mother had said. And Mikey looked at the palms of his hands and hurried to wash them.

He hated the blackness that covered his father's hands. Sometimes as his father prayed over the dinner table, Mikey kept his eyes open and watched his father's hands. They were black all over, and the nails were stubby and split. He didn't want them to touch him. But his brother and sisters didn't seem to mind. They let him rub his dirty, ugly hands over their heads when he came home from work, and when the praying was over at the table, his father ate with those hands. Mikey watched to see if any blackness rubbed off on the soft white bread, but it never did.

Mikey didn't want hands like his father's. His father's hands were those of an ignorant man, those of a man who helped fuel the coke ovens at Capital. They were the hands of a man who worked by the canal, at the coal stockpiles.

"Why don't he wash his hands?" Mikey once asked his mother when he was five.

"He do wash them," his mother said.

"Then why they never clean?"

"Your father work hard, you know," his mother said. "He don't got no easy job over 'cross in that plant, no clean job. So what, he ain't got no pretty hands. He got the hands of a working man."

"I'm not going to work in the plant when I grow up. I'm never going to have ugly hands like Daddy," Mikey said.

His mother slapped his face. "Don't you badmouth your daddy, boy. Don't you know I'll slap you into the middle of next week? What's wrong with you, boy? Your daddy a honest man, not like some 'round here that wouldn't take a job on a pie train. Don't you never let me hear you say nothing bad about your father again or I swear before God I'll wear you out."

Mikey did not say another bad thing about his father, but he meant what he said. So when his mother said, "Your hands look like your daddy's," he went into a silent panic and rushed into the kitchen to scrub them.

It was only ink that covered Mikey's hands, though, newspaper ink that had rubbed off when Mikey folded his papers in the living room. But Mikey couldn't even stand that. He had to wash the blackness off, and once his hands were clean, he rinsed the blackness from the soap.

"It's already a quarter to four. You don't want to be late," his mother was calling from the living room.

Mikey dried his clean hands and went out front to load

the papers in his wagon. This was his first day. He was the first black boy the *Buffalo Star* had given this route to, but he was unimpressed. And as he began his route through All-Bright Court with his load of papers, he thought, It's no big deal.

Halfway through his deliveries a shout came from behind him. "You new on this route?"

Mikey turned, reluctant to have his back to whoever was speaking to him. Just the week before, a meter reader from the gas company had been shot in the back on this block. Everyone said that Isaac did it, that he was strung out and needed the money for a fix. But the man had only three dollars on him.

Mikey saw Isaac every morning. As Mikey waited on Ridge Road for the bus to Buffalo, he saw Isaac and some other young men in front of the new liquor store that was opened on the site of what had been Dulski's. They would be there when he went home in the afternoon, standing in the same positions as when Mikey left.

"Hey you, paperboy," the shout came again.

An old man was on the porch of 125. He was wearing blue boxer shorts and a pair of yellow open-toed ladies' slippers.

"Yes sir," Mikey yelled.

"Where my paper?" the man asked.

Mikey walked over to the man's porch. He looked harmless enough.

"What happened to that Polack boy?" the man asked.

"I don't know, sir. I think his family moved away from here."

" 'Sir, sir.' What's this 'sir' shit? And that white boy brung me my paper first. He delivered this row 'fore that one you was on."

Mikey handed the man a paper. "I guess I came in the opposite direction, sir."

"Seem like you should know my name. That white boy knew my name. And I knows yours. You the Taylor boy. I's Woodrow. Shake my elbow."

Mikey backed up a step. There was liquor on the man's breath. He smelled as if he had been beaten with a juniper bush.

Woodrow took a step forward with his elbow out, and Mikey looked at the man's feet. His toenails were yellow and curled under. Mikey thought they looked like the claws of some sneaky woodland creature.

"Go on. Shake it."

Mikey shook his scaly elbow. "I'm Mikey Taylor."

"I told you I knows you. I worked with your daddy in the plant when he first come up here. That been years. You wasn't no bigger than a June bug when I first saw you . . ."

Mikey was no longer listening. He stared around Woodrow and into the house. "Didn't someone else used to live in this house?"

"What, you crazy, boy?" Of course other people lived in this house. You think I just come up from Mississippi and they built this house 'round me? Who you thinking of?" Woodrow asked.

"I don't know," Mikey said. "There was a boy and his mother."

"You talking 'bout that nasty woman that had that boy what was killed. She been gone for years. Where the hell you been, boy? Somewhere with your nose in a book?"

"It's just that I just thought of it. I —"

"I give up fish," Woodrow said.

"Pardon me?" Mikey said, having trouble following the drunk man's logic.

"Pardon you? What you think I is, a priest? I said, I give up fish. I caught me some fish out there on the lake last week and froze them, and when I took them out today, you know what happened?"

Mikey did not say anything.

"I say, you know what happened?" Woodrow said, raising his voice.

"No."

"They come back to life, was swimming 'round in my kitchen sink, boy. I'm telling you, I caught hold of those bastards and threw they live ass out the back door. That was a sign from God," Woodrow said.

"I have to be going," Mikey said.

"I'm telling you it was a sign from God," Woodrow said, but Mikey was already backing away.

Mikey thought about Woodrow's fish story as he continued on his route. It shouldn't have surprised him, he thought.

These people were so backward, always full of fantastic stories, trying to add a dimension, an invisible plane of magic. It was sad, really. They told fantastic stories because they had nothing, were nobody. They had to spin stories out of the air because they had no magic in their lives, no gods or myths. They were not at all like the Greeks and Romans who Mikey learned about in school. They had done nothing to civilize the world, to add to its history and culture. Why, there was only one black man in Mikey's whole world-history book, Hannibal. And it was said that maybe he wasn't black. He could have been a Moor.

These people in All-Bright Court reminded Mikey of a girl in his class at his old school. Every day this girl came to school wearing the same faded purple cotton dress. If she did not have that dress on, she had on a pair of worn green pedal pushers and a yellow cotton blouse with tattered sleeves. And she had a story. "I got nicer clothes at home. A whole closet of all kinds of pretty dresses and things, but my mama won't let me wear them to school."

This was how these people were, talking, talking, talking with their closets full of nothing.

18

COVETING

HE WAS Venita's son, mornings. Gloria would bring him to 92 wrapped in layer upon layer of blankets. Each day when Venita peeled back the layers she was amazed anew. It seemed to her he was an angel. When she lifted him from his covers she half expected to find a pair of wings entangled in them. Black ringlets covered his perfectly round head, and his soft and coppery skin shone where Gloria rubbed olive oil into it.

Gloria had married an older man, a man who worked at Capital, cleaning the company offices. She had married him three years after Jesús left. It was said that Jesús had been seen in Buffalo. He was living in his cousin's store, had gone to Canada, to New York City. There were rumors he was coming back, that he would show up for the wedding. But he never did. If he were coming back, he surely would have come earlier, when Gloria was dating *un jíbaro*, fresh off the boat.

That man's name was Regalo, and he claimed he could trace his heritage all the way back to Ponce de León. His bloodline was unbroken and led through the centuries to the night Ponce de León had lain with Regalo's greatest of grandmothers. The sky, moist and warm, had pressed on him like a damp sheet, and hours after Regalo's greatest of grandmothers was gone, Ponce stayed awake listening to the coquís sing. It was said, even then, that only the male frogs called out. That was the night Regalo's greatest of grandfathers knew he would go searching for the fountain of youth.

Gloria thought Regalo was the saddest man she ever met. He would disappear for weeks, trapped in silences he could not break out of, and without explanation he would appear again. He wanted to go back to Puerto Rico, he would tell her. When his family had moved to America, they went on welfare. It was a source of shame for Regalo; his family had descended from such lofty heights. On *la isla verde,* if they could not have money, if they could not have happiness, they could at least have warmth and the coquís singing in the countryside. Gloria thought the place he missed must be heaven, and Regalo was an angel who had stumbled and fallen to earth.

The first time he hit her, she knew he was human. She had given him a cup of coffee that was not hot enough for him, and he had slapped her. She had let it go. He had not meant to do it, he said. It would not happen again. But that was how it began, and when she could no longer hide her bruises from her parents, they forbade her to see him. "He's crazy," they told her.

But even the crazy need love, and she loved him. "Coming to America made him crazy," Gloria told her mother.

"He was probably crazy before he left Puerto Rico," Gloria's mother said. "There are crazy people there. Once there was *un tabaquero* whose daughter ate her own flesh. She bit off pieces of her fingers. Crazy."

Although Gloria was forbidden to see Regalo, she snuck him in when her parents and César were not home. But one evening he began beating her, and she ran from the house. She escaped out the back door, and he chased after her.

The Taylors were eating dinner, and through the screen door they could hear Gloria and Regalo coming toward their back door. Gloria kicked and fought her way onto the Taylors' porch. Mikey jumped up from the table. Samuel moved toward the door, but before he could get there Gloria and Regalo had fallen against the screen. The door came loose from its hinges and crashed into the kitchen.

The door hit the floor first, then Gloria, face up. Regalo landed on top.

Mary Kate and the children were screaming, crowded in the doorway between the kitchen and living room.

"What the hell is this?" Samuel said. "Get out of my house."

Mary Kate calmed down enough to ask, "She dead?"

"She don't look dead to me," Samuel said, "just knocked out."

Regalo had gotten to his knees and was trying to revive Gloria.

He kissed her and kissed her while he knelt among the scattered and broken plates, the pinto beans, corn bread, half-eaten chicken.

"She dead!" Mikey yelled. "She dead!" And he ran upstairs.

"Take them kids out of here," Samuel yelled.

"Get them out of here? They in they own house," Mary Kate yelled back. "Where you want me to take them? Get *them* out my house!"

Samuel glared at her. "What you want me to do?" he asked. "You can take them kids upstairs."

Regalo paid none of them any attention. He had begun to cry.

Samuel looked out of the space where the door had been. A crowd had gathered, staring into the hole, right into the house. Samuel stepped over the couple and yelled at the people gawking outside. "What ya'll want? Get out my yard."

Nobody moved. They were not scared of him.

The children had quieted down, and Mary Kate went to the sink, wet a dishcloth, and handed it to Regalo. Gloria was coming around. She opened her eyes and Regalo picked her up. Without a word he carried her past Samuel, nodding to him as he went out of the hole.

"Who going to pay for this shit?" he yelled after them.

"He going to kill that girl if this keep up," Mary Kate said.

No one would have been surprised if Regalo had been found stabbed to death, Jesús having snuck back to kill him.

But Gloria had had enough. She stopped seeing Regalo. He would still come around, a coquí crying out in the night, but she would not answer his calls. Finally, only an arrest kept him from coming back.

He had been riding the bus from Buffalo, and when it was time for him to get off on Ridge Road, he did not have the ten cents to exit in the suburban zone. So, although other people had their exit fares, the driver refused to stop at the last three stops on their side of the bridge.

"I'm sick of you people doing this," he said. "The whole lot of you always wanting something for nothing. No more. No more." He drove the bus right over the bridge to Capital Heights, pulled up across from the police station, and began honking the horn.

When two officers in front of the station approached the bus, Regalo panicked. He tried to kick out a back window but only managed to crack it. By this time the officers had walked around to the front of the bus, and when the driver opened the door to let them on, Regalo rushed the door. The officers grabbed him and dragged him struggling from the bus, across Ridge Road, right into city hall, and down to the basement headquarters.

Regalo was charged with disorderly conduct, destruction of property, petty larceny, resisting arrest, and assaulting two police officers.

Gloria started dating a new man. The neighbors were still apprehensive. "I don't know why I got the damn screen door fixed," Samuel said.

There was no need to worry. The new man, who had white hair, was named Orlando, and Gloria had met him at a Saturday night bingo game at the Our Lady of Assumption Church on Ridge Road. The games were conducted bilingually, but Orlando was illiterate in both English and Spanish. He came to bingo to socialize, and sat smoking and drinking coffee while the games were played.

Gloria would look up to catch him staring at her. Every week he sat closer. At first he was across the room, but with each progressive week, he moved a table closer and held his stares a little longer. When Gloria stopped dating Regalo, she began to return the gaze of this white-haired man.

Because Orlando worked night hours, cleaning the offices at Capital, he seldom saw Gloria during the week. He met her mother for the first time at bingo.

He was respectful, addressing her mother in Spanish, and he offered a small gift, a bar of chocolate. Because of the chocolate, Gloria's mother thought Orlando must be a pervert.

When she had been a girl there was an old man, *un abacero,* who owned a small candy store. He had given chocolate to her friend Mercedes, a very dark girl, thin and quiet. He let her eat as much chocolate as she wanted. Once she had eaten ten bars. To pay for them, she would sneak out and come to him at night. The old man would slip his penis into her mouth.

Gloria's mother put the chocolate Orlando had brought in her purse, but threw it out when she and Gloria got home. "I don't like that man," she told Gloria. "He is trying to buy you."

"Mommy, buy me? With what?"

"I don't like him. He is too old for you. An old man like him should be ashamed. He could be your father," her mother said.

"Mommy, he is not that old."

He kept bringing small gifts to Gloria's mother, a bottle of soda, peanuts, a ripe avocado. One week he brought her a piece of sugar cane three feet long. Finally, she invited Orlando to come home with them and share it.

Gloria's father peeled the cane and gave everyone a piece. Gloria never had cane before. A sweet and milky juice that reminded her of coconut milk ran down her chin. The rough fibers of the cane bit at her tongue.

"I chopped so much as a boy, I thought I'd never want to see a piece of this again," Gloria's father said, sucking on his fourth piece. "Sometimes for days it was all we ate."

"It's not as sweet as in Puerto Rico," Gloria's mother said.

"It's good," Gloria's father said, "but nothing is as sweet as that."

Gloria and Orlando were married in a civil ceremony at the city hall four months after they met. Gloria's mother cried through the entire ceremony. César and Gloria's father attended. Regalo was there too, still in the basement jail. He was supposed to have been moved to the county holding center in Buffalo, but there was no room for him yet.

The day prior to the wedding, Gloria's mother had given her some advice. "You're a smart girl. You could get a good job, be a secretary. Live some of your life. You have a choice.

Work until you have children. Have something to fall back on because children can be disappointments."

Gloria listened to her mother's advice, stored it away. But her mother did not know. Like so many women, she had not had the chance to explore the world. Her place, their place, was at the shore, pressed against the sea. Their men had explored the seas, discovered the roundness of the world. Gloria's mother did not know where to tell her to go, or how to get there. All she could do was stand at the shore and point. A woman who has never been into the world thinks of it in two ways, finite or infinite, ending at the horizon or stretching on forever. Gloria's mother believed in its infinity. But Gloria was afraid to try, to become a disappointment. A month after the wedding, she was pregnant.

Gloria's pregnancy was easy. Orlando would come home from work early in the morning and tend a small garden he had planted in the back yard. Gloria would sit there too, inside the chicken-wire fence he had put up. Like his garden, Gloria was ripening. Her thick hair was growing, beginning to inch down her back. She was rounding out, her legs and arms growing bigger, her face filling in. Her breasts grew. These mornings in the garden, her breasts were like avocados he could rub for luck. But he did not touch her. He refused to touch her.

Gloria did not know what to do. She tried to cover her confusion, but her mother saw right through it. "Is he beating you?" she asked. "If he is beating you, I will kill him."

"It's not like that," Gloria said.

"He's doing something to you. *Hijo de puta*. You should not have married him. Nothing good will come of this marriage."

"Everything is fine," Gloria said.

"Why are you lying to your mommy? Don't you know it's

a sin to lie to your mother?" she said, stroking Gloria's hair.

Gloria began crying. "Orlando, he won't touch me. You know, *touch* me. I don't think he loves me."

"Is that all?" her mother asked. "Don't cry for that."

"He's my husband," she cried.

"My *niña*, I know he's your husband, but don't you cry. Orlando loves you. Sometimes men act strange when a woman is expecting. When I was carrying Jesús, I thought Poppi was crazy. He wouldn't let me do a thing. *He* cooked, *he* cleaned. Ay! He brought me breakfast to bed. I thought I was a queen. That was with Jesús. By the time I had you and César, he knew better. He treated me like a woman with you two. I cooked, cleaned, everything."

"It's embarrassing," Gloria said. "It's like I did something wrong . . . Maybe he has another woman."

"Ha!" her mother yelled. "Who would want him? He is lucky to have a girl like you. He knows that, and when the baby comes he will be all right. You'll be glad for these days. When the baby comes, he'll go back to treating you like a woman."

All summer the plants grew up around Gloria. The onions, the peppers, the tomatoes. The tomatoes were threatening to take over the entire garden. They were leaving no room for her. Orlando would walk past her like she was a ghost and tend to the needs of the plants, pulling weeds, turning over leaves looking for bugs, hosing down the garden if there had been no rain.

Toward the end of the summer, on a morning before Orlando came home from work, Gloria flew into a jealous rage. During a light rain, she rose from the stool where she sat, spotted a tomato plant near the fence, and tried to rip it from the ground. It was choked with green and red tomatoes, and it fought her, unwilling to give up its life.

As Gloria was struggling with the plant, a woman came around the corner in a mad dash. It was Venita, in search of a piece of salt pork for Moses's breakfast. She had set out for Mary Kate's house, hoping she would have some. In her haste she had forgotten her scarf, and between the rain and her husband's demands for pork at six in the morning, her hair was going to go back. She was in no mood.

When she saw Gloria pulling on the plant, though, she stopped. "What you doing, girl?" she asked.

Gloria started and let go of the plant.

"If you trying to pick tomatoes, that ain't the way," Venita said. She approached the fence. "You got some fine ones here. I'm in a rush now, but I'm a come back by later and give you something for some. How much you want?"

"You can take some," Gloria said.

"That's kind of you, but I can't let you do that," she said, pulling a few green ones from the plant. "I want these, and I'm a get some to put up. I'm a pay you, hear?" Venita said, and continued on to Mary Kate's.

Venita came back later with a dollar and a bag, and Gloria told her to take as many tomatoes as she wanted. "You should start putting some of these up," Venita said. "The frost's coming soon and they going to go to waste. The peppers too. You got a green thumb. This is a fine garden you got here. I can't make nothing grow."

"It's my husband's," Gloria said.

Gloria's mother was right. When the baby was born, Orlando went back to treating her like a woman. And he loved his son. They named him Miguel.

Each morning when Orlando came home from work, Gloria would be in the kitchen and sometimes Miguel would be awake, lying in a basket in the center of the table. If he was not awake, Orlando would go upstairs and get him.

"*Enamorado,* he's tired," Gloria said. "You're going to spoil him."

"You always say that, honey. But I never see him. He's always sleeping."

"He's a baby. He needs his rest."

"Look at him. Can you believe it?" Orlando would say, holding the sleeping Miguel.

Miguel was four months old when Orlando was laid off. Along with severance pay he was given a slip of paper in an envelope. He took it home for Gloria to read to him.

"It says this next week will be your last week. They're cutting back on the cleaning staff."

"My last week! How can they fire me?" Orlando said. He was holding Miguel, who was asleep.

"*Mira,* you weren't fired. They're cutting back. Half of the cleaning staff is being let go."

"How will the place be clean? Half the men! Pigs. It's so dirty. Cigarette butts, coffee cups everywhere. Piss on the bathroom floors. They run around in those suits, looking all nice and neat. Big shots. But they're pigs. What do they think I'm suppose to do, just like that?" he said, snapping his fingers. "Sending out these little pieces of paper in a envelope. At least they could have faced us like men. *Maricóns.*"

"We will make a way," Gloria said. "My parents can help."

"I don't want them to help. You're my wife, and I'll take care of you and Miguel. I will get another job," Orlando said.

Nearly two months passed before Orlando found a job. A Puerto Rican man could always find a job mopping a floor or scrubbing a toilet.

But Gloria found herself being pulled out to sea, water swirling around her ankles.

"I was thinking, Orlando. About going back to school," Gloria said one night as he was preparing to go to work.

"Back? You finished school."

"Not high school, business school," she said.

"Why do you want to go to college?"

"Not college, Orlando. I could be a secretary. Already I can type forty words a minute. I could when I graduated."

Orlando was not listening. "You think I can't take care of you and Miguel. That's why you want to work. You want to take over."

Gloria was stunned. "That's not true. I was thinking that I could, that I might —"

He yelled at her. "You don't think I'm good enough for you. I'm nothing but a *casero*, cleaning up piss and shit. You want one of those *blancos* sitting behind one of those fancy desks, not the man who cleans up after them."

"That's not true," Gloria yelled back at him. "How can you say something so crazy? Trying to push me into the arms of a white man."

"You should've married one, somebody who could give you something. With me you will never have nothing."

"You give me all I need. You're mixing up what I'm saying. I'm thinking about the future. Maybe we can send Miguel to college. Being a secretary is all I think I can do. It's all I think I can be good at. You're good at cleaning."

Orlando laughed bitterly. "I'm good at it. I can't read. I can't write in two tongues. I'm a stupid man. That is what makes me a good janitor," he said.

"Orlando," she said. "You are a man. I take pride in your work. You take pride in your work."

"It's not pride I take *in* my work. I work hard, do honest work. That is what I take pride in. But it is not enough. *Mi padre* worked and took care of everybody, us kids, Mommy, a brother too. I have trouble feeding just three mouths."

"That was Puerto Rico. It's not the same now, here. Nothing works for us here. Here we pay, pay, pay. Water, food, big rent, heat. Bills, all the time bills. And what do we get? Hell, we pay for a sewer that backs up in the yard."

Gloria was accepted at secretarial school in downtown Buffalo, with enough grant money to cover the cost of the yearlong program. There was one problem: what to do with Miguel. Her classes started at eight A.M., but she had to leave Lackawanna by seven. Now that Orlando worked nights in Buffalo, he did not get home until eight.

"I'll get someone to keep him mornings," Gloria told Orlando. "Maybe the lady in back of us."

"Her? She has twenty-seven kids."

"Don't be silly. Mrs. Taylor is a nice woman. She keeps her kids nice."

"I don't know," Orlando said. "Where will she put *mi niño?* When it's time for his nap, she will have to put him on a hook."

Gloria decided to ask anyway. Venita was at Mary Kate's when Gloria came by. She had Miguel with her, hanging from her hip. Though Gloria spoke to Mary Kate, Venita jumped in. "I'll keep him. Can I keep him?" She reached for the baby and he went to her. "See, he like me, with his pretty self. Girl, you got you a pretty baby. He a angel."

"He's no angel," Gloria said. "You'll see that."

"You mind, Kate, if I keep him?" Venita asked, and before Mary Kate could answer, she turned to Gloria. "I know you ain't asked me, but I want to keep him. I'll do it for free."

"Gloria, I think you should let Venita keep your baby. If the truth be told, I can't really take him on, and she good with kids. She love them."

Venita's morning son began coming the next week. The first morning, Venita tried to sit and hold him, but he was eight months, too big for that. He climbed out of her lap and slid off the couch. He explored her living room and kitchen, and Venita was amazed that he kept finding things. She thought her house was clean, but suddenly he would be chewing, and when she pried his mouth open, she would find a tiny pebble, a grain of rice, a button.

Venita told Gloria about Miguel's ability to find things when Gloria unexpectedly picked up the baby herself one afternoon.

"I told you he wasn't an angel," Gloria said.

"Yeah he is, and he fast. You got to watch him like a hawk. I don't let him get into nothing. Where your husband?"

"He didn't wake up. I hope it wasn't a problem, me getting here later," Gloria said.

"It wasn't no problem. Don't feel like ya'll got to rush to come get him."

Gloria did not fully understand what Venita had said. For, though Orlando was supposed to pick up Miguel at noon, sometimes he would come before then, as early as nine or ten, cutting short his morning's sleep to spend extra time with the baby.

Venita did not go to Mary Kate's house when she was watching Miguel. She did not want to share the little time she had to spend with him. Miguel was too busy exploring his new world to pay much attention to the woman who had mistaken him for an angel. But Venita did not notice. She was content to follow him through the living room and kitchen, snatching danger from his hands until he began slowing down. Miguel seemed to have a clock in his stomach. He knew he had a ten o'clock bottle. Sometimes, before Venita took it from the refrigerator he was there trying to open the door.

This was the only time Miguel would let Venita hold him.

She would sit on the couch, rocking back and forth, pressing him to her breast, playing with his curly hair, singing to him.

She had tried singing "Mockingbird," but she wasn't sure of the words. "If that diamond ring don't shine, Mama going to buy you a bottle of wine . . . A bottle of wine? That can't be right," she had said. "What mama would buy her baby a bottle of wine?" She could not think of anything to rhyme with "shine," so she sang "This Old Man" and "Old MacDonald."

Mary Kate did not say anything, but she missed Venita, wanted her to come over for starch and gossip. She would look out the window of the back door, lifting the curtain.

"Who you looking for?" Dorene had asked her one day when she had come home for lunch.

"Nobody," Mary Kate had told her. "I was just looking."

"She coveting that child," Mary Kate told Samuel one day.

The morning before Thanksgiving, Orlando picked up Miguel at Venita's at ten, took the baby home, and then lay on the couch while Miguel played with blocks. Though Orlando had had a short nap, he was exhausted. The long bus rides, the staying up nights, the work, and the cold were all wearing on him. Orlando's eyes closed.

Miguel crawled away from the blocks and headed for the kitchen. He stopped along the way to put a piece of string in his mouth. In the kitchen, he opened the cabinet under the sink and pulled out two cans of food. Behind them was a bag of beans.

They were fava beans. The plastic bag was torn open and the beans had spilled onto the shelf. Miguel sat before the cabinet and picked up one of the tan, pebblelike beans. Gathering beans in both hands, he stuffed his mouth until it could hold no more. Then he swallowed. Three beans fell from his mouth. Two slipped down his throat.

As he began to gag, his tongue shot out, sending another

bean falling to the floor. But the two beans were still caught in his throat. Unable to make a sound, he fell over on his side, a bean still clasped in one hand. He curled up, just as if he were asleep.

Orlando awoke to Gloria's screams, but it was too late. The baby was dead. Before the ambulance came, Orlando shook Miguel so hard to try to wake him, he broke his neck.

Mary Kate called Venita, and without a coat, Venita ran out of the house. She and Mary Kate were among the crowd that stood in Gloria's front yard. When Venita saw the baby's body carried out of the house, covered in a sheet, she sank to the ground. Mary Kate tried to pick her up, but she couldn't. A man from a few rows over carried her to Mary Kate's house as Gloria was being brought out on a stretcher. Orlando followed behind, no longer a man, barely a statue.

Venita blamed herself. Gloria blamed herself. Orlando blamed himself. Gloria's mother blamed him too. She accused him to his face. "If it wasn't for you, *mi nieto* would be living. I hate you. You killed Miguel. *Asesino. Asesino.* I'll see you in hell before I send my Gloria back to you."

Mary Kate later told Samuel, "A flavor bean, favor bean. I ain't never hear tell of such a bean the baby choked on. Gloria fell out, and Venita, she fell out, like somebody struck her with a bolt of lightning. She blamed herself. But it ain't nobody fault."

"Naw, it ain't nobody fault," Samuel said.

"Venita was the one all the time carrying on like that baby was hers," Mary Kate said. "You don't run 'round getting attached to other people kids. Don't nothing good come of it."

19

COLLECTING

MIKEY could see the man's breath cloud and dissipate before him in the night air. He could feel it and smell it. Warm, almost hot, and redolent of oranges. The man wore a black ski mask. As he held a gun to the side of Mikey's head, he said, "I should kill you. You think you somebody, don't you?"

Mikey did not know if he should answer. He thought it was a rhetorical question. "You think you somebody?" the man asked. "Answer me, paperboy."

"No, I don't think I'm somebody," Mikey said.

"Good. 'Cause you ain't nobody. You ain't nothing. Hear me? You not shit, boy," the man said. "You been collecting for your papers. Well, I'm collecting too." He ripped the full coin changer from Mikey's belt and stuffed it under his jacket. With one big, shaking hand, he searched through Mikey's pockets.

The sweet smell of the man's breath was making Mikey

sick. He tried to block it out, tried to block out what was happening to him by forcing the scene out of his mind. He ground his thoughts to dust.

From the dust came a vision of the man with the gun as he came toward him through the field. He was walking left of the narrow path of packed snow. His head was bowed and his hands were in his jacket pockets. He kicked up the deep snow as he walked, and as he silently passed, Mikey thought, I know this guy. That was — But a gun at his temple interrupted his thoughts. The man's fragrant voice said, "I should kill you."

And there was a summer field of dandelion and Queen Anne's lace. Mikey and his father were crossing the field. He was only three, and they were eating Popsicles from the Red Store. Orange-colored sweet juice dripped from one of his father's blackened hands and into the dirt along the dusty path. Mikey could see the orange drops leaving brown dots as they fell in the dust. And from the dust rose the man's sweet voice. "Get out of here," he said. But Mikey stood and looked at the man. "If you tell, I'll kill you," the man said, his voice echoing in the thin winter air.

Mikey took off along the slippery path. Running toward home, he thought, I know him. That was Isaac. Then he fell, the ground seeming to come up to meet him. He tumbled into the whiteness of the field, coming to rest face down in the snow, its coldness numbing him. He expected to escape the terror of this nightmare and find himself in the warmth of his bed. But he was awake in the bed of cold whiteness, and he did not know where Isaac was. Mikey leapt up from where he lay, expecting the gun to reappear. His foot became tangled in the buried weeds as he started running. He stumbled, but kept his balance.

As Mikey ran, kicking up clouds of snow, Isaac's words

came back to him. "If you tell, I'll kill you." With each stride he moved farther and farther from the field, grinding Isaac's sweet words to dust. By the time he rounded the row to 18, there was nothing left for him to tell. He had ground Isaac's words to a fine powder that blew away in the wind. There was no robbery, no gun. There was not even Isaac.

20

HOODOO

IN THE CLOSET under the stairs at 79, the albino girl lay and dreamed. She dreamed there was a door at the end of the sloping closet, a small door. Through the door came a black boy. He was small when he came through the door, but once in the closet he was big and he sat with his knees to his chest. The boy had come to bring the albino girl color. He had come with a small tin of watercolors.

He opened the tin and painted her soft, fat, white body. The boy painted with short, quick strokes that felt like the licking of a cat's tongue. He mixed the colors and painted her black. He used them all up to make her black.

The girl was allowed outside then. She could be seen. The wind blew on her and the sun shined. Its light did not hurt her eyes. She was loved. Her mother and father loved her. The boy loved her, and she and the boy danced. There was something in the dance that summoned rain. It fell like a punishment and washed the color away. The rain made her ugly again, and she ran back inside. She hid in the closet, and the boy followed her. He told her he would bring color again. He would go home for crayons. "They won't wash away," he said.

And the boy made himself small again and went back through the small door. But before the boy could come back, the colorless girl awakened.

She awakened to find the door at the end of the closet had disappeared, and she had been sleeping. She had been hiding and dreaming in the closet because she was not loved. Her parents believed this child was punishment. She was a spell worked up by her grandmother.

"She working a spell," Zena's mother said when Zena told her of Greene's kindness.

"She never even talked to you before. Why should she start now?" her mother asked.

"Because I'm having Karo baby. It's her grandchild," Zena said.

"I'm not sure that's not a spell too."

"Oh, Mama," Zena said.

"Don't you 'oh, Mama' me. You was too young to remember when Greene first come up here. That was the summer them bats came. She was country, country, had them funky asafetida tied 'round them kids' necks."

"I remember that Karo used to wear one," Zena said.

No one could ever remember Greene's children being sick. They never got chicken pox, measles, whooping cough, mumps, not even a cold. Most children stayed away from them because the bags gave off such an odor, but Zena did not.

It was Zena who convinced Karo to take the stinking, dirty bag from his neck back in 1966.

She came near Karo. She danced the Willoughby with him. She held his hands for pop the whip.

"It's stupid," Zena said to him. "It don't really protect

you from germs. That's country. You know the school nurse
say ya'll don't get sick 'cause don't nobody come in breathing distance of ya'll. Why don't you just take it off?"

This and Zena's smile were all it took for Karo to break
the string and throw the bag away.

He told his mother the string had broken and he had lost
the bag in the field. Greene said nothing. Karo was almost
twelve anyway. He didn't need it anymore. But when he
went to sleep, Greene sat on the edge of his bed and raised
the lids of his eyes to find Zena dancing in the back of them.

Greene never disliked Zena. She was never nasty to her,
but she was not nice either. Sometimes Zena would appear
in Greene's house, just like air, just like she had always been
there. Greene never spoke to her. How could she speak
to air?

Zena's mother could not keep her away from Karo, so she
warned her about Greene.

"You stay from out her house, you hear?" her mother
said. "And don't be eating nothing she cook. I mean nothing. Ain't telling what she might cook up in it." Zena's
mother said Greene cast the evil eye. Greene caused the sewers to back up, caused the winters to be harsher and the
rivers to rise higher in the spring. She could raise ringworms
and mange on children's scalps. She could even make husbands cleave to her and not to their wives. The men came to
her seeking treasure. And the bats had come with Greene's
arrival. They had come only that one night, and they had
never returned. That could not be ignored.

Zena and Karo married in 1972. She was pregnant, and
though Karo was only eighteen, Greene signed for him to
marry. He went off and joined the navy.

In Zena's fifth month she became sick. Her stomach was
upset and her urine turned dark. There was a milkiness, a

whiteness, that passed across her irises. It drifted slowly, like a thin cloud against a windless night sky. After two days of sickness, Zena admitted to her mother she had eaten at Greene's. She'd had some potato salad and collards.

"She working a spell. I'm telling you, she working something on the baby. She done something to mark the baby," Zena's mother said.

"That's crazy, Mama. That's just a bunch of country talk."

But Zena never felt right after her dinner at Greene's. She was always tired, and there was an uneasiness inside her, a cold whiteness that moved from Zena's eyes and into her womb. The baby seemed to pick it up. It made the baby still.

The doctor at the clinic said there was nothing wrong, but the birth of the baby proved the doctor wrong.

She was a fat white baby with white hair and pink lips. All of the color had been washed from her.

Karo had been out to sea when the baby was born, and when he came home and saw her, he refused to hold her. He did not even want to touch her. The baby was ugly, Karo said, and Zena kept her hidden in the house. Both of their families shunned the child, but Greene had come over to see her once.

She came to bring an asafetida bag for the child. She tied it around the baby's neck, and told Zena, "I knows what these people be saying about me, but it ain't true. I ain't no conjure woman. But how can you tell people that? People believes what they want to." That was the most Greene had ever said to her, and before she left Zena's house, she repeated, "People believes what they want to."

Zena took the bag from the baby's neck and threw it away, and for five years she kept the child hidden.

Mikey had managed to see this all-white child, though.

He had seen her far off in the darkness of the afternoon house, her milky blue eyes staring at him as he opened the screen door and placed the newspaper on the floor inside.

After her nap on this day, after the colorless girl awakened to find the door at the end of the closet had disappeared, she went and sat in the cool darkness of the living room. When she heard the paperboy coming up the porch stairs, she went to the screen door.

He opened the door and stared at the child's white skin, her woolly white hair, her full pink lips. He smiled at her and handed her the newspaper.

Though he had not come from the closet, she thought he was the black boy from her dreams. Her milky blue eyes moved rapidly as she tried to focus on the boy. But the brightness of the afternoon sun took her vision away, and the boy became a shadow.

"Do you have the crayons?"

The boy was confused, and before he could answer, the girl's mother was there. She was floating above her, just like air. She struck the child, knocked her to the floor. The sheets of the paper spilled over her, and the screen door slammed.

"I told you to stay away from the door. No one want to see you. Don't nobody come here to see you," her mother said.

It seemed as though talking to this child hurt Zena, as if with each word she were spitting sand.

Mikey saw the girl get up, her mother's hand printed pink across her face. Before he left the porch, he saw the girl run from the door and disappear into the closet under the stairs.

21

———~———

LITTLE SNOW, BIG SNOW

"LITTLE SNOW, big snow. Big snow, little snow." This was what people said of winter storms. It was a way to gauge the strength of the storms, to predict the change they would bring.

Big snow fell in large, wet flakes. There was an openness, a boldness to it. And the snow fell slowly, floating down lazily from the fast-moving clouds overhead. It could fall all night, but by morning the storm would have waned, and there would be little snow on the ground. A snow that brought about a change just small enough to be beautiful, just big enough to be an improvement. A trace covered the dead grass, a dusting covered the naked branches of the trees.

Little snow could fall for days. It fell in tiny, light flakes driven by strong winds and brought big amounts of snow. It was the subtleness, the diminutiveness of these flakes that could deceive. Storms that carried them could start with a disinterested flurry slipping in from the lake. And at first, they too brought beauty, a softness. But when the snow didn't stop, the beauty was destroyed. As the snow rose, it began covering up, obscuring, hiding. The kind of change that came with little snow had been working in Mikey since he had begun attending Essex.

Early on, what Mikey was learning seemed to bring about a beauty in him, a softness. He was put in a speech class where he was taught formal conversation. He listened to tapes entitled "Verb Tense," "Possession," "Agreement." He learned to release his vowels, to round them and pop them out of his mouth. It seemed unnatural to him at first, and he felt almost a little guilty, a little embarrassed when he practiced retaining his -*ing*'s.

"Think of it as a game, like juggling eggs," Mikey's speech teacher had said. "If you keep them all in the air, you'll dazzle the audience, but if you drop one, you'll make a mess."

Mikey kept his teacher's analogy in mind, and practiced not dropping his -*ing*'s.

No one at school dropped them. None of the boys were constantly making messes of themselves. Mikey listened to them speak in class. He heard the joking in the cafeteria and the locker room. In these two places it seemed a boy could make a mess, a boy might be expected to make a mess. But the other boys never dropped their eggs. The two older black boys he had seen never dropped their eggs either, even when Mikey saw them speaking to each other.

Mikey wondered at them, he wondered about them. He wondered if they had ever spoken like him, and where it was they came from, and how it was they looked so comfortable. They spoke with no effort, it seemed, when he had to think about everything he said. Mikey wanted to sound like them, to look like them, to walk up and down the halls with the white boys and talk about skiing and sleep-overs. But both of these boys were in the seventh grade, while he was in the fourth, and they appeared each day with short, neatly brushed hair that had very little grease. And they showed a remarkable talent for juggling.

It was Mikey who dropped his eggs. It was Mikey who broke enough in one sentence to make himself an omelet.

"Practice" is what his speech teacher told him. "Practice at home when you speak with your family members."

And that was what Mikey did. At the dinner table he would not say, "We be havin' fun in gym class," but "I had fun in gym class today."

Or, "When I was riding home today with Mrs. Cox, I saw a tanker out on the lake."

Dorene would tease him. "Listen to him talk with all that proper talk. All the time now you be trying to talk like a white boy."

But his parents would come to his defense. "Just cut that out," one of them would say. "Ain't nothing wrong with the way he talk. That's the right way to talk. The rest of ya'll should try to talk that way too."

Mikey's parents were proud of the way he spoke. He was smart and getting smarter, sounding smarter. They never corrected him when he made a mistake. They didn't know how. His parents could both see the learning was changing him, but so was the unlearning.

They did not know that during his second semester at Essex, Mikey had told a boy what his father said about monkeys.

Mikey was six when his father told him. They had been in the monkey house at the Buffalo Zoo. His mother had refused to go inside, and waited out front with Dorene and Mary.

Inside, his father said, "I'm telling you, don't pay no attention to they screaming. They smart, smart enough to talk. But they won't, 'cause if they do, they know white people going to make them work."

"Is that true, Daddy?" Mikey asked.

"Yeah, it's true. My daddy told me so."

Mikey had repeated the story to a boy named Scott in the school cafeteria. They had been studying evolution. He was careful to watch his diction, and censor the part about white people. He said only, "People will put them to work."

But Scott laughed at him. He laughed so hard, he spat out a mouthful of butterscotch pudding.

"You're not serious, are you?" he asked. "Your dad isn't really stupid enough to believe that?"

"No," Mikey said. "It's just a story he told me. Please don't tell anybody."

"Why not? I think it's funny," Scott said.

Despite Mikey's request, Scott repeated the story to the whole science class. Even the teacher laughed. "That's an amusing story, Michael. We all know primates have intelligence, but they have not evolved quite that far yet," the teacher said.

Mikey was embarrassed, but he kept it covered. He kept it covered at home, too, when his father asked what he had studied at school that day. He told him they had studied evolution.

"Man didn't come from monkeys. Don't let them white people tell you that. If they want to believe they came from monkeys, fine. But don't you believe you came from them," his father said.

"But we were studying Darwin, and he says —"

"Don't tell me what he say. I know what he say. I'm not stupid, you know. Sometime I think you don't believe nobody got sense but you. If you so smart, answer me this. If man came from them, why there still monkeys? And what monkeys turning into?"

"I don't know," Mikey said.

"You think them monkeys in the zoo turning into men?"

"I don't know," Mikey said. "No. No, they are not becoming men."

His father said, "Damn right. They smarter than men. Laying up in zoos all over the world, got white men feeding them. Just because they in them cages don't mean they don't got no sense," his father said, and he laughed.

And Mikey wanted to tell him. He wanted to say to his father, "You're not really stupid enough to believe that!" He wanted to take his father's laughter away. He was smarter than his father, and he was angered by his stupid, trick questions.

Mikey did not understand that his father was not laughing at him. He was laughing at the beauty, the simplicity of his fresh-faced cocoa boy.

"I know you got to get a education, and I want you to have one. But just don't believe everything white people tell you, son," his father said. "With all you education you still going to be a black man in a white man's world. Sometime the only thing you going have is your beliefs."

Mikey only half listened. His attention was focused not on what his father said, but the way he said it. He had dropped all of his eggs. There was no subject-verb agreement. His father was a stupid man who did not even know how to speak. He was a man with yolk dripping from his chin.

As Mikey continued with his education, he was more careful. He brought home little of what he learned in school. Just like all those years ago when he had seen the circus clown pulling the seemingly unending string of scarves from his mouth, Mikey had begun pulling silences from his mouth. His silences were not long and silken. They were perfect ovals, each popping out smoothly and unbroken. His parents did not know because he did not live in silence. He never stopped speaking, though he ceased talking.

Every school day Mikey was set free from a world adrift and sent into the other world. He did not have to search over open water for a place to rest his foot. He did not go out and bring back an olive leaf. He was supposed to have it with him every day before he left home, to have the waxen greenness firmly clamped between his teeth. Just as he had turned nine, he was made an ambassador and an example of what was good and right and white about black people. Mikey became afraid of doing the wrong thing, of saying the wrong thing.

Neil Armstrong had walked on the moon the summer before Mikey went to Essex. His father had said, "That's all a trick, son. That man ain't on no moon."

When the subject came up in the school cafeteria that fall, Mikey did not say anything until he was addressed directly. He was concentrating on slicing a piece of rubbery baked chicken, fighting the urge to pick it up, when one of Scott's friends said his uncle was an aeronautics engineer who had worked on the *Apollo 11* mission.

"Mikey, wouldn't it be neat to be an astronaut?" the boy asked.

Mikey swallowed a piece of the tasteless chicken. "Yes, it would be neat to go to the moon, or even another planet."

"That would be neato," the boy said. "My uncle said in ten years men will go to Mars. I want to go."

"Me too," Mikey said.

"Hey, Mikey," Scott said. "I bet your dad doesn't think man even went to the moon."

"No," Scott's friend said. "He thinks monkeys went." Scott and his friend laughed.

Mikey laughed too. He did not respond to what the boys said. While he sat slicing his chicken, he thought he was betraying his father, and he knew he had to hide this betrayal. At home he would be silent. He would never mention this conversation. It would be as if it never took place.

As Mikey went back and forth between the two worlds, he knew he had to hide the ignorance he brought from home, the truth he brought from school. He collected these truths and lies one by one, beginning with monkeys and Darwin and astronauts, and swallowed them. As they began gathering, filling him, he began pulling silences from his mouth.

He had not had to do much. As his education progressed, it took on a voice of its own that ran interference in his conversations. His father rarely questioned him about his work. Once Mikey had reached the sixth grade, Samuel understood little of what Mikey was doing, but his mother would ask to see his papers or spelling lists. She came across words she had never seen before — connotation, divination, torpor, mensuration, alchemy, codify, zygote.

"What's this 'zygote'?" his mother asked him one day when he was in the seventh grade.

"Well, it's sort of — what it is, is a cell that represents the union of two gametes," Mikey said.

"Oh," his mother said. She had no idea what her son had just said. Though she had been pregnant many times, she never knew a zygote was inside her. She would have been angry if she knew someone accused her of carrying around something that had such an ugly name.

"Oh," his mother said again. "You better get ready to take your papers. I folded them already."

She never asked about "mensuration." "Do mensuration problems," he had written in his notebook. She only wondered why they were teaching him about a woman's monthly.

Mikey was watchful about what he brought to school from home. Once he unpacked his backpack in front of his locker and a roach crawled out. Mikey could only stand there. He was too afraid to move. If anyone noticed, he would surely know it came from him. Mikey wanted to run after it, to smash it before someone saw it. But no one saw it, and Mikey watched the roach disappear through a crack.

From that day on, Mikey shook out his backpack before he left home. He shook out his books, and if he was wearing a coat, he shook that out too. And he started a bathing ritual.

Every Sunday night he sat in the bathtub for an hour. He washed his hair, and soaped his body twice, and scrubbed it with a rough cloth. He wouldn't have any odor coming from under his arms, no hint of musk from between his legs, no smell of rancid grease in his hair.

He went to school like the two older black boys, with his hair cut short and severely brushed and ashy. Even when the other boys in All-Bright Court were getting blowouts, and wearing their hair in a bush, Mikey kept his short. He did not care that the other boys called him a square and a Tom, an Oreo, a faggot, a sissy, a fool.

"What you think you going to be?" the boys in All-Bright Court teased him. Mikey would never answer.

"He think he going to be the President when he grow up," they would say. "Well, you ain't. You ain't going to be no more than the white man going let you be. You just like us. You ain't no better than us."

Once Mikey's father heard the teasing, and he took up for Mikey.

"You damn right," his father shouted out the front door. "He going to be the goddamn President of the goddamn United States if that's what he wants to be. What ya'll going to be?" he asked, breaking into a fit of coughing.

But the boys would not answer.

"You got to stick up for yourself. Ain't nothing wrong with having dreams," his father told him, catching his breath.

"I don't know if I have dreams. All I want to do is get out of here," Mikey said.

"That ain't much of a dream. There worser places than this. You got a chance I never had, a chance ain't hardly no black man ever had. You take this education you getting, and you make something out of it. Don't be afraid to dream, son. Them boys out there afraid to dream. Even rabbits dream. Even when they living 'round a whole lot of foxes. They still go to sleep and dream how to stay ahead of the foxes, and when they wake up, they try. That's all I'm asking you to do. I want you to try. And when you get your ass run ragged, I want you to get some rest, and get on up and try again."

"All I want to do is get out of here," Mikey said. "We're living in a cage here."

Mikey did have a chance to get out, to move away little by little. He would be invited for sleep-overs. He would go to Williamsville, Amherst, Tonawanda, Cheektowaga, West Seneca.

His parents didn't want him to go to the white neighborhoods. The first time he was invited to Cheektowaga his father said, "What you want to go out to some white-boy house for? Don't they have black boys at that school?"

"I've told you there are, but Scott invited me to his house.

I've been at Essex for almost four years, and this is the first time I have been asked to sleep over. Dorene said she'll take my papers on Friday," Mikey said.

"It ain't the papers, son," his mother said. "Those white people don't want black people out there. You know that. Why can't your friend come here?"

"Because it's not just me. He invited some other boys also. I've been *invited*, Mama. All the boys in the eighth grade do it."

"You ain't 'all the boys,' son," his father said. "Sometime I think you forget that. Sometime I think you forget you black."

Mikey said, "Well, sometimes I want to forget. I don't have any friends around here. Now you want to tell me you don't want me to have friends at school. You want me to dream, and you want me to know my place. That doesn't make sense. It's a contradiction."

"That's the world, son. I don't make no sense, but I didn't make the rules. You ain't got to believe what I say. You go on out there to Cheektowaga," his father said. "I'm through."

Mikey did go. And he was glad Scott did not come to his house. When he saw Scott's family's house, he knew why he could never have Scott or any of the other boys come to All-Bright Court.

Scott lived in a home, not a house. There was a den, a pool out back. There was a family room, a living room, and two and a half baths. And there was a shower in the full bath that Mikey used. They had only bathtubs in All-Bright Court.

It was the first time Mikey ever took a shower. At school there were showers in the locker room, but only the boys on the sports teams could use them. As he stood in the shower, the water danced on him, tickling him, and he laughed out loud.

When he got out, Scott asked, "We heard all that laughing. What were you doing in there?"

"Nothing," Mikey said.

"You're a strange bird," one of the boys said.

But Mikey did not care. He couldn't let them know that was his first time in a shower. He would never live it down.

And Mikey went ice skating. It was his first time on skates, and he spent most of his time crawling around on the ice while the other boys whizzed by him. But by the end of the session, he was slowly gliding around the rink. After skating they walked to a pizza parlor, and later that night they went to a movie theater.

On Sunday afternoon when Mikey returned home, there was a sullenness in him. His father did not say anything to him. He knew what was wrong. He knew Mikey found out not everyone lived as they did.

He had been *invited*, and he had been treated well. That's what was important, Mikey thought. And he was invited again, to other boys' houses, and on ski trips and campouts. But sometimes he was not treated well.

Once when he was roller-skating in Hamburg, near Buffalo, a boy from town tripped him. And in Amherst he had been called a nigger while he and his friends were standing on line outside the Dairy Queen. His friends consoled him, saying, "Don't pay any attention to that."

How can I not pay attention? Mikey thought. But he covered up, and popped a smooth silence from his mouth. "Sticks and stones," he said.

But the name-calling did hurt, and he heard it almost everywhere he went. It did not happen every time, but just as he was relaxing, just when it seemed he was one of the boys, someone would call him a nigger, or call his friends nigger lovers, or tell him to go home, to go back where he came from.

Mikey never told his parents any of this. He told them what a great time they had at Kissing Bridge, and never told them that after skiing, while his friends talked to girls, he played pinball or sat before the fire in the lodge. He didn't tell them he had been dunked at the town pool in Williamsville, that two white boys had held him under until he thought he would drown. He didn't tell them that he'd told the lifeguard, who said, "That's what you get for coming to where you don't belong."

If Mikey told his parents any of this, they would have stopped him from going. He just knew they would. They might even take him out of Essex.

His parents were baffled by his new life. Mary Kate said, "Mikey say Scott father going to teach him to curl. What's that, Sam?"

They were lying in the darkness of their bedroom. "You seen it on TV, on the Canadian channel. That's when they be sliding them rocks down the ice —"

"And they got them handles on them, and then a man run down the ice and sweep it fast with a little broom," Mikey's mother said. "That's stupid. He already ice skate and ski. It seem like he only want to do what the white boys do."

"The boys 'round here don't do much of nothing," Samuel said. "That what you want him to do, nothing? Grow up and work in the plant, if he lucky. 'Cause they still cutting back every day, you know that, and there ain't no telling what the new contract going to bring."

"I just worry."

"Well, you the one wanted to send him to that school," Samuel said.

"Me? Me?" Mary Kate said, the pitch of her voice rising. "You wanted him to go too. I was the one worried."

"Don't get flighty on me now. It was both of us. What was we going to do, hold him back? We had to let him go."

"Yeah, I know that, but I don't know if we done the right thing," Mary Kate said.

For a while Samuel was silent. "I don't know if we done right either. They is giving him a good education, and he going to go to college," he said, and he began coughing.

"It seem like he changing too much. All he want to do is be 'round them white boys from that school. It seem he turning into a white boy. The only thing black about him is his color," Mary Kate said.

"Sometime it seem that way," Samuel said quietly. "But, he ain't getting all that education to come back to the projects, nohow . . . Part of that D.O.V.E. program is to get black kids mixing with white kids. You can't get black and white mixing as grown folks and think things going to work out. There's truth in that, Kate. How many white friends we got?"

"Why you ask a question like that when you know the answer?"

"None, that's how many," Samuel said.

"That don't prove nothing. What, we got to have white friends to be happy?" Her voice was defensive.

"Here you getting ready to argue with me. Kate, don't argue with me, hear? All I'm trying to say is, the boy got his own life. I be scared to let him sleep at them white boys' house, just like you. Me and no white boys was ever friends, never could be, and you wasn't friends to no white girl."

Mary Kate was silent.

"This ain't the world we growed up in. Sometime I don't

know what to tell Mikey 'cause I don't know the world he living in." Samuel started coughing again.

"You need to see a doctor," Mary Kate said. "Your cough don't sound like it's getting no better."

When he stopped, he said, "What a doctor going to tell me that I don't know? I'm a be all right. Mikey the one I'm worried about. You know, the boy told me he don't got no dreams. All he want to do is get out of here, get as far away as the wind can carry him. What can we do?"

22

NO ONE HOME

NO ONE KNEW how long she had been there alone, swimming through the blue silence of the house. She made no effort to leave the space that confined her.

Mikey was the first to know she was there. For three days, when he had gone to deliver the paper to 79, he saw the paper from the previous day. On the first day he paid little notice, but on the third day, when he opened the screened front door the other papers fluttered and blew apart at his feet. How rude it was, he thought, for Zena to go away and not tell him to stop delivery.

Mikey had come to expect little from these people. There was a customer who lived on the last row, in the very last house, whom he had had to cut off. The man would not pay on time. When Mikey went to deliver, the man was always there, and always said, "You late, boy."

"I'm sorry," he would answer.

"Don't be sorry, be on time," the man would say.

Zena was a good customer, though. She always paid her bill. She had gone away before, but on those occasions she had told Mikey or left a note for him.

The day Mikey found the papers was a Thursday. He did not return until Sunday, collection day. When he knocked on the door and no one answered, he turned to leave. But before he could step off the porch, the door opened. He turned to see the colorless girl.

She stood in the door, looking up at him, her blue eyes moving rapidly from side to side, trying to get a fix on him. He so rarely saw her when he delivered or collected that he had nearly forgotten about her. She would be lost so deeply in the blueness of the house that it seemed as if she had wandered through a wall and was living her life as a ghost.

Her eyes made him uncomfortable, and he asked, "Is your mother in?"

"She gone," the girl said.

"When is she coming home? I need to collect."

"I don't know. She been gone."

Mikey looked beyond the girl, into the stillness of the house, to see if Zena was somewhere back there, if she had sent the child out to lie for her.

"I seen you," the girl said.

"What?" Mikey asked.

"I seen you put the papers in the door."

"I didn't think anyone was here. Why didn't you come out and get them?"

"There wasn't nobody home," she answered.

He glared at her, though she did not seem to notice. "*You* were here," he said. "You just told me you saw me."

"Wasn't nobody home," she said, casting her eyes away.

It was time for Mikey to move on. He could not waste the afternoon talking to this child.

At dinner that night, slicing into a piece of fried chicken, he mentioned what the girl had said. "She kept saying that no one was there, but *she* was there. She's been there all this time. She was weirding me out."

His brother and sisters looked at one another and laughed.

"What's funny?" Mary Kate asked. "Ya'll think what he said funny?"

"No ma'am," they answered in unison.

They all thought their brother was turning white: eating fried chicken with a knife and fork, saying "weirding me out."

Samuel said, "I don't want to be the one to say it, but I think the child mama done run off."

"It don't sound right," Mary Kate said. "And come to think of it, I ain't seen the mama here lately."

"I haven't seen her recently either," Mikey said, "but that doesn't prove anything. You are jumping to conclusions."

"Yeah," Dorene said, "and it's weirding us out." She and the other children laughed again.

"They're making fun of me," Mikey said.

"Ya'll stop laughing at ya'll brother," Samuel said.

"Well, he shouldn't be talking like that. What he say be funny," Dorene said.

"Shut your smart mouth or I'm a send you from the table," Mary Kate said. "Can't even have a peaceful Sunday meal without ya'll yapping like a bunch of puppies." Once the children had settled down she said, "It's dangerous for a child that age to be left alone. Anything can happen, but it ain't none of our business."

"You right," Samuel said. "But me and Mikey run 'round there after dinner. If we don't go, you ain't going to leave it alone."

"I'm a go too," Mary Kate said.

"Naw, you expecting, and I don't want you going. You never know," Samuel said.

"Samuel, it's a child."

"I say I don't want you going, and I mean that. You stay here. Me and Mikey ain't going to be gone but a bit."

The door to 79 was closed when Samuel and Mikey approached. Samuel knocked and waited. Knocked and waited.

"She's hiding from us," Mikey said. "Let's go."

The door opened.

"That's her," Mikey said.

Samuel glared at him. "What you think, I'm blind or stupid?" He turned to the child. "Where you mama at?" he asked in a gentle voice.

"She gone."

"I know," Samuel said. "How long she been gone?"

"A good while," the girl answered.

"What's 'a good while'?" Mikey interrupted. "Can't you give a time estimate? One, two days?" She did not respond. "See what I mean, Dad?"

"Shut up, boy. Let me handle this," Samuel said.

"She been gone a good bit," the child said.

"We going to take a walk to your grandma's, hear?" Samuel said.

Mikey looked up at his father. "You're taking her to Greene's?"

"Who you think you is, calling grown folks by they Christian name? Next thing I know, you be calling me Samuel. Come on," he said to the girl.

The girl stepped out of the house, and the brightness of the day caused her to squint.

She walked alongside Samuel, stumbling over the uneven sidewalks. Mikey lagged behind. He could see women, their heads popping out of windows, women stepping onto porches, wiping their hands, hands on hips, hands pointing. He knew they were watching, for walking a few steps ahead of him was the embodiment of a spell, walking around like a real child.

Mikey did not believe in black magic, but he was embarrassed to be seen with this imitation white child. He did not believe she was the product of a spell. There were no spells, no magic, no hoodoo. Life was reason with no rhyme. Mikey did not know that while ghosts were being vanquished during the Age of Reason on the Continent, the ancestors of his people were performing magic, building a nation of brick and stone, of wealth and power, out of bolls of cotton. They had no reason to discount magic when they worked it every day.

Greene was on her porch churning ice cream, looking quite ordinary, surrounded by four of her boys. Samuel did not exactly know what he expected her to be doing, but this was not it. Who thought of a conjurer making ice cream?

"Good evening," Samuel said.

Greene stood up and cast her eyes down on them. A milky film covered her left eye, and though Mikey tried to not look, he was drawn to it. It was the eye of a snake.

"Hot enough for you?" Samuel asked.

"It ain't never been hot enough here for me," Greene said.

One of her sons took off the top of the freezer. "Mama, it's ready," he said, pulling the paddle from the cylinder. Another child, another boy, came from the house with spoons and a stack of chipped bowls.

"Ice cream?" Greene asked. "It's peach. I would eat some myself, but all that cold make my teeth hurt too bad."

Before Samuel could answer, Mikey said, "Yes, please," and a bowl was passed to him.

Samuel could not remember Mikey ever wanting Mary Kate to add peaches to the ice cream she made. He always wanted vanilla. Yet here he was eating, of all things, fruited ice cream stirred up by a witch. And then there were Greene and her children, acting as if the girl were not there. Samuel had to look down at the child to make sure she was.

He was damned if he'd be stating his business out in the yard. "Can we step inside?" he asked.

"Sure thing," Greene said.

Once they were in the house, Samuel got to the point. "You see, I got you grandbaby. I know it ain't none of my business, but I brung her here 'cause she say her mama done run off."

Greene reached into the pocket of her housedress and took out a small, rusty red tin. She took a pinch of its contents and placed it inside her lower lip.

"You right, Mr. Taylor. It ain't none of your concern," she said, placing the tin back in her pocket. "And I got news for you. If you brung Clotel here for me to keep, you can keep walking with her. I can't keep her. Times is hard, and I ain't got no extra, nothing to feed her, no place to put her. If you leaves her here, I'm a have to turn her over to the state." Though her voice was flat, underneath it was sadness sewn as finely as a blind stitch.

"You thinking I'm a hard woman, ain't you?" she asked.

Samuel did not look at her. He looked around the room at the yellow walls, the pots of food on the stove, the dishes piled in the sink. How ordinary it seemed. This could be his house.

"Her other grandma live in Buffalo, over in the Fruit Belt, on Grape Street."

"Can I get the number?" Samuel asked.

"There ain't no phone," Greene said.

"I see," Samuel said. "I know you ain't got no car. I could take the child over there, run her by there tomorrow."

Greene got up from the table. "Let me get the address," she said, and she left the kitchen.

Samuel glanced out the door. The child was sitting on the sidewalk, her knees drawn to her chest.

Greene came back with the address written on a piece of brown paper bag. "All a body can do is what it can, Mr. Taylor. No more," she said, handing the scrap of paper to him.

Samuel left the house. "Come on," he said to Mikey, and he picked the girl up.

"What's going on, Dad?" Mikey asked.

"Shut up," Samuel said.

Mary Kate, Venita, and the children were crowded on the back porch when they arrived.

"Open the door, Martin," Samuel said.

Everyone filed into the kitchen and Samuel placed Clotel down. The children gathered around her. She stood looking at the floor, her eyes moving, searching under the pink lids, while the children stared at her.

"It's a white girl," Mary said.

"She ain't white," Martin said.

"All ya'll get out of here. Every last one of ya'll get," Mary Kate said. "Staring like ya'll ain't had no upbringing."

Samuel pulled a dollar from his pocket. "Mikey, take them all to the store. A dime apiece, and bring the girl back something."

They scrambled out of the kitchen, and Mary Kate went to the stove to fix the girl a plate.

Clotel ate everything with her hands, corn bread, chicken, green beans, tomatoes. While she ate, the adults went into the living room, and Samuel spoke softly to the two women about what Greene had said.

"You shouldn't have went in the house," Venita said.

"She right. You shouldn't have. She could of put something on you," Mary Kate said.

"She didn't," Samuel said.

Mary Kate said, "I don't know, you come back here with a child."

"Don't you start with me, now," he yelled. "She was going to turn the child over to the state!" He began wheezing.

"Ssh," Mary Kate hissed.

"I shouldn't of went there period," he said in a lowered voice. "I promised to run her to her other grandma, and then I'm through with it. This what you get for sticking your nose in where it don't belong."

"Well, she can't go to her grandma's looking like this," Venita said, and while the other children were out, she began cleaning up Clotel.

As she filled the tub with tepid water in the bathroom upstairs, she pondered her feelings for this child. Clotel did not have baby Miguel's beauty, his copper skin, his shiny curls. She was no angel, though she lived her life unseen. This was a child who needed someone to look after her, and if Venita did not do, who was going to do?

Venita bathed the child and washed her hair and put her down in a bottom bunk in the girls' room, where Clotel cried herself to sleep. The women went and sat out back, where Olivia, Mary, and the youngest child, Jonetta, were playing hand-clapping games.

"We brung Mary Janes for the white girl," Jonetta said.

"You call her by her name," Mary Kate said. "Your daddy say she Clotel, and you call her that, and she ain't no white girl. Mary, you go find Dorene and Mikey, and have them get started on them dishes."

Venita sat picking at her nails.

"You all right?" Mary Kate asked.

"Yeah, girl. I was just thinking. What kind of mothers women are these days."

The next morning Mikey woke up sick. Mary Kate went to see about him, and Martin said, "Mama, he ate at Miss Greene house yesterday. He say he ate ice cream."

"He what?" she yelled. "Samuel! Samuel!"

"Kate, you going to wake up the whole house," Samuel said as he was coming up the stairs.

"I don't care if I wake the dead. That boy ate at Greene's?"

Samuel hung his head.

"He did, he did, didn't he?" Mary Kate screamed, her voice high-pitched and strangling.

"Before I could stop him, he did. What was I supposed to say after he accepted? Say, 'Hey, boy, don't be eating nothing from that woman'?"

Mary Kate went back to Mikey and Martin's room. Mikey had the covers pulled over his head. He wanted to disappear.

"What can you tell that boy? He think he know every damn thing," Samuel said from the hall.

"Well, he don't. You happy now, boy?" she asked Mikey. "You believe in her power now? I'm a dose you with castor oil. That's all I can do."

All day Mikey lay in bed, sick and sulking. His stomach was queasy and his mother was ignorant. Why did she insist on walking through darkness when she could walk in the light?

Clotel had not gotten up either. Lying awake, balled up in a corner of the bed until after nine, she thought she must be dreaming, and her stillness kept the spell from being broken. If she moved, she would awaken in her own bed, her mother never having left, the paperboy never having come. Until Venita came over to ask about her, Clotel stayed in the bed holding on to the dream. Even as Venita dressed her, gave her a bowl of cereal, she was not quite sure if she was awake.

After breakfast Venita pressed Clotel's hair. Clotel sat perfectly still, even though the heat and anger of the comb was right on her scalp.

"She hold a good head," Venita said.

"Olivia hold a bad head," Mary Kate said. "Don't you, baby?"

"Yes ma'am," she said. She was sitting on the floor playing jacks. "I don't like no straightening comb. When I grow up, I ain't going to straighten my head."

"When you do that, don't come to my house, you hear? You ain't running through my house looking like no African," Mary Kate said.

"I ain't going to straighten my hair either," Dorene said. She was standing in the doorway between the kitchen and living room, already beginning to look like a woman. "I want me a afro, a big bush."

"Girl, you old enough to know better. Venita, tell this child she too black to have her head nappy."

"Your mama right. Don't no black man want a nappy-head black woman, especially not a dark-complected one."

"Well, they should marry white women, then," Dorene snapped.

"Don't get sassy," Mary Kate said.

"Mama, even you said that before. When Daddy be complaining about you pressing our hair, saying he ain't like all that loose hair flying through the kitchen, 'cause if some of it got in his food, and was going to grow in his stomach."

"You ever heard of such foolishness?" Mary Kate asked.

Dorene continued, "And you be telling him he should of married a white woman if he don't want no hair in his kitchen. And beside, you be burning our hair, right?"

"Right," Mary Kate said. "Down home we say, you burn your hair that fall, 'cause if you throw it out and a bird get hold of it and make a nest out of it, you'll go crazy."

Venita left after Dorene and Mary went to deliver Mikey's papers. She had made a tuna and macaroni salad for Moses, and she needed to fry some livers and gizzards before he came home. She was going to ride over to Buffalo with Sam and Kate when they took Clotel to her other grandmother.

Moses didn't like the idea when she had told him the night before. "What happen to that child ain't none of your business. Why you going, getting tied up with somebody else child?" Moses asked.

"Moses, she a good girl. I straightened her hair and combed it. We just going to run her over to Buffalo, that's all. Who going to do?" she asked. "Her mama might never come back."

"What kind of mama is she, anyway? Leaving like that," Moses said. "People want children, and other people be throwing them away like they nothing."

Moses and Venita rarely spoke of children. It was too upsetting. The topic was closed, like her womb. Moses did not blame Venita, though. He would have liked to have children, to have the white silence that enveloped their lives chipped away, to have the sound of a child's voice break through its shell.

So they danced around the awkward silence their stopped conversation had created, but Moses and Venita knew that this child would not be wanted by the people she belonged to.

"I just don't see why you got to go," Moses finally said.

"I ain't said I had to go. Mary Kate don't drive, and Samuel don't want to take the child by hisself," Venita said.

"So he taking two women along with him. For what, protection?"

"What you got against Samuel?" Venita asked.

"Nothing. He don't like me, think I'm a cotton-picking, collard-green-eating, shuffling, Uncle Tom nigger."

"Please," Venita said. "He not like that. He a lot like you."

"You got a hole on your head, woman. That man ain't nothing like me. You go on to Buffalo, put your nose in where it don't belong. I don't care," Moses had said the night before.

But when Moses came home from work this late afternoon, when he entered the muted silence of the house, he changed his plans.

"I want to ride over there too," Moses said while he washed his face in the kitchen sink.

"What for?" Venita asked. "I won't be gone but a little while." She looked at him warily.

Standing at the sink with water dripping from his face, Moses threw out an excuse. "If you want to go, it's my place to take you. I ain't going to have that man driving my wife nowhere, showing me up. I ain't riding with Sam Taylor, neither. I'm taking my own car."

Venita said, "It don't make no sense to take two cars. I'm riding with them. I done told Mary Kate, and I'm not going back on my word. How would that look?"

A knock on the door settled matters. It was Samuel.

"Moses going to ride with us," Venita said, cutting her eyes at her husband, "if that's all right with you."

Naw, it ain't all right with me, Samuel wanted to say, but instead he said, "Suit yourself."

Moses and Venita climbed in the back seat. Moses said, "Mrs. Taylor, Mr. Taylor," and tipped his straw hat to Mary Kate and Clotel, who were in the front seat.

Samuel pulled the car onto the pike. No one spoke. The radio played softly, all the windows were down, and the car filled with a moist breeze as they drove past Capital, heading north along the lakefront.

The Fruit Belt wasn't hard to find. It was only a half mile off Main Street, on the east side. The farther Samuel drove, the worse the houses looked: old two-story wood-frame structures, leering under peeling paint, threatening to slide off their crumbling foundations.

These houses were like the old houses on the streets near All-Bright Court. These streets like those streets. Change the height of the buildings, the width of the streets, and you could have been in any ghetto in the North, in New York City, Chicago, Detroit, Philadelphia, Newark, Pittsburgh, Cleveland. If you turned into the east side, north side, south side, west side, uptown, or downtown, wherever it was black people had been pushed and crowded together, you found people who had come up from the South seeking to fulfill their dreams and had stumbled into an unending nightmare.

A swarm had gathered on Grape Street. Samuel could drive only halfway down the street because the crowd blocked his way. He parked the car.

"We need to go further down. We ain't nowhere near the house," Mary Kate said.

"What you want me to do, Kate? Drive through these people?" Samuel said. "Ya'll stay in the car. I'm a go down the block to see if they home."

He opened the door and got out. Moses got out of the back. Samuel looked at him and started off down the block.

The two men walked down the street like they were

strangers, and each took a different path through the crowd. Somewhere near the center they both emerged into an opening, and there in the street, flowing down the slightly inclined slope, were thin veins of blood, all emanating from one source, a drying puddle, and the people had gathered around as if they expected it to speak.

Samuel and Moses pushed on, each stepping around the blood. Moses followed Samuel until they stopped in front of a house. Two patches of dirt framed either side of the short, broken front walk. The steps that led up to the house were rotted through.

"Hey," Samuel called to a girl on the porch. She did not look much older than Mikey, and she had a baby welded to a thin hip.

"Ya'll some kin to her?" she asked.

"Who?"

"That woman what was killed," she said in a disgusted voice.

"Is your mama home?" Samuel asked.

"My mama?" the girl said, sucking her teeth. "This my house."

"I'm looking for the Hargroves. I was told they live here."

"Well, they don't," the girl said.

From the neighboring porch an older woman yelled, "Them people been moved."

"You know where they went to?"

The woman came down from the porch. "Them people moved back south. Can you blame them? All this craziness. That woman got shot this morning. She lived just over there," she said, pointing across the street. "Wasn't up here a year good, from Georgia, Mississippi, Alabama, someplace. Her husband chased her out into the street and shot her. I was sitting on my porch trying to catch me some air when he come running out screaming something crazy about some half-cooked pork or some such foolishness. He blewed the top of her head clean off. Her brain come right out the skull, and that fool didn't even run. He dropped the gun and sat right on the porch till the police came and took him. They took the kids too. They was hollering, Lord, they was hollering. I don't think the mama or daddy had no people up here. It's a horrible thing when you ain't got no people. Them children being turned over to strangers. I done took eight aspirins since this morning, and I still got a headache. I wish some of these people would go on home. Half of them don't live this way. They just come to be nosy, mind other folks' business," the woman said, and quickly added, "I don't mean ya'll."

Moses was still standing behind Samuel. The men briefly glanced at each other.

"Ya'll together?" the woman half stated, half asked.

For a moment they were silent, and then they each said, "Yeah."

"Yeah," the woman said. "Them people been gone."

On the way back to the car Moses followed Samuel, skirting the edge of the crowd. A crowd like this could be there whenever you turned onto a street like this on a hot summer afternoon, and the woman who told its story would be there too, perpetually descending her steps, speaking in tongues, telling the story of the drying blood while the sun slid west.

Moses stopped and caught Samuel's arm. "We can't just give that child away," he said.

Samuel stopped, but he did not look directly at Moses. "I don't know how I got dragged into this in the first place. I'm telling you, I don't want to believe Greene a conjure woman, but I don't know."

"What we going to do with this child? Stop downtown

and put her off at city hall, the county building, wherever?"

"Why you keep saying 'we'?" Samuel asked. He stood with his hands in his front pockets. "It seem like that's what *you* would want to do, let some white folks wind up with her, take her into some nice home, and let me tell you something, it might be the best thing for her."

Moses shook his head. "You been waiting all these years to say something like that, ain't you? You think you know me, but you don't, and let me tell *you* something. I'm trying to live, just like you. We been working like dogs all these years, and between us, what we got? Manage to save some money and all you can get is a house like these here."

Samuel did not answer. He looked at Moses fully, something he had not done for nearly fifteen years. Moses's hair was turning gray; his eyes were yellowing. In that moment he could see an old man rising through his skin. Half of his life was over.

"Seem like we come all this way just to die," Samuel said, and began walking.

Moses walked alongside him. "Stay black and die," he said. "That's what my mama used to say whenever my daddy told her she had to do something. She would say, 'Ail I *got* to do is stay black and die.'"

They shared a laugh steeped in bitterness and sorrow, and as they approached the car, they could see Mary Kate and Venita standing alongside it. Each was fanning herself with a handkerchief. Clotel was in the front seat, sleeping.

Before the women could ask what happened, Samuel said, "Them folks gone south. We going to take her back to Lackawanna. Ya'll get in."

Mary Kate and Venita looked at each other. "We heard about the shooting," Venita said. Both women got in the back seat. Moses pushed the door closed behind them and he sat in front. Samuel got in on the driver's side and lifted Clotel to Venita in back.

They were headed down Main Street when Moses said, "Me and Venita going to take her home, look after her till her mama come back. What ya'll think?"

"It's for the best," Mary Kate said, looking at the child stretched out over herself and Venita. Clotel's head was in Venita's lap, and Venita stroked her hair. The child flushed bright pink, and as the car cooled down, the color faded from her face.

They drove on in silence, but that silence was comfortable. There was nothing that should have been said.

They got on the pike, drove past Capital's offices and the plant along the lakefront. The smell of sulfur burned the air. From the stacks, endless plumes rose and drifted over All-Bright Court.

When they came to the turn at Holbrook, Moses said, "They say if you stay on this road it'll take you all the way south." And they turned off.

23

JOURNEYMAN

THE LETTER to Henry read:

What you doing, man? Long time no see. I bet you never expected to hear from me again. I didn't know what had happened to you. You never know with a war. I should of wrote. I been writing you for years you know how that be. Everyday you going to do something tomorrow then you going to do it the next day then the next thing you know you wake up and its been years. Its been years, man. I been in and out the navy you knew that? Maybe you knew that. My mama saw your mama so maybe you know. I was a cook. Ain't that about a blip? Me a cook. It got my ass out of Nam I tell you that. Man I been everyplace. Hong Kong, Hawaii, Guam, Australia. They got brothers in all them places some chicks too. I ain't got no love for the navy. Join the navy see the world. I saw the world from behind a steam table. I ain't complaining you know things can always be worse. But you get sick of being told what to do. Some dude mad at you at 6 in the dam morning because he don't like the way the eggs look. Shit I'm telling you, man. You be done got up a hour before his ass and you don't like how the eggs look neither and the way they smell cause you got a hangover. I'm telling you man, cooking wasn't shit. When I felt like it I spit in the fucking pots, so I cut hair. That was where it was at. Money. You know them jacked up monkey hair cuts they make you get in the service and they got some white boy that ain't never seen a brother before basic let alone cut they head. So I got me some clippers and went to town. Money, let me tell you. I charged them dudes $2 a head all the while thinking that when I got out I was going to open up a barber shop. But let me tell you man, while I was out seeing the world every negro and his brother was getting a fro. Can you beat that? Get off that ship for the last time look at them brothers walking around LA. Thought I was on another planet. So I say the hell with being a barber I'm a be a hairdresser and let me tell you there a gold mine in black women heads. A gold mine. There plenty sisters with nappy heads but there plenty of them that come in regular once a week. Come to the shop more regular them they go to church. You know me I can slap some chemicals on a head send them naps running. You should think about coming out here to LA, man. The west coast bad. No snow. Its where its at I'm telling you. Fuck the east. The east ain't nothing. Out here things cool. Don't no white dudes hassle you. Not like them crackers back east. There ain't no crackers out here, I'm telling you. White dude come over the mountains with a attitude a hundred years ago them indians killed they ass. White people know better then to have a attitude here cause there enough niggers and Chicanos to kick some serious ass. Chicanos is west coast Portoricans but badder. They got attitudes and guns and they want something they get it. They cool you know like brothers. Them crackers back east think they got something. Them people living on the other side of the bridge. I'm telling you I rent now but when I get my house its going to be nicer then they houses. They got brothers out here live in mansions. Man, you know who I saw out here? Some boy named after syrup. Karo. I wouldn't of known his ass from Adam. But I was in this club where some brothers in the service hang out, and he was there with this white chick he brung from Germany. You know when a black dude with a white chick he got to be seen, so he got to talking to me about this and that, you know. There's a lot of brothers out here with white chicks. But I still like my coffee. Know what I'm saying? I'm a get my own shop too. The service good for something. A loan, you know. I'm working in this dude shop now trying to get my own customers. This dude take half what I make. Half. I'm telling you he missed his calling as a pimp, all his money go up his nose. He a fool. But I bootleg, do some heads out my kitchen. You got to do what it take. But I ain't write to say all this. I was thinking you should come on out here. You going to want to stay. I'm warning you about that. Be cool and write me and let me know.

Be cool,
Skip

Wait I forgot to tell you something. I'm sending you something. A surprise.

Later

The next week the package arrived, an afro wig, balled up like a small, black, hibernating animal, along with a note:

Hey man how you like it? Its made out of plastic so don't be putting it in no hot water and whatever you do don't be near no hot stove in it.

"You should write that boy back," Henry's mother said.

"He not a boy, Mama. He a grown man like me, and I don't know why you say write him. You never liked him," Henry said.

"That's not true. I ain't got nothing against the boy, never did. When I saw his mama, I give her the address to send to him. If I had something against him, I wouldn't have done that."

Henry said, "He doing real good, Mama. He want me to come out there."

"I think he a blessing. Lord knows I never thought I'd say that 'bout Skip. You should go on out there, though. This sure ain't the place to be. You know Isaac was arrested on the other side of the bridge. They say he was robbing a house."

"He should know better to be over there," Henry said.

"What he going to steal over here? Ain't nothing over here, unless he was going to steal one of these kids running 'round here," Henry's mother said. "Yeah, you should get while the getting good. But is you going to wear that wig?"

"I don't know. Skip say brothers out there be wearing them," Henry said.

"I bet *he* say that. What is it with that boy and hair? I still ain't forgot the time he put that process in your head, the slick-head fool," Henry's mother said.

"I'm a go," Henry said.

"I got a dream of going out there one day. Skip mama been out to see him. Watts is where she say he at. She say black folks living good out in California, got fancy houses and cars, making barrels of money."

Henry said, "That's what Skip say."

24

RESURRECTION

ZENA CAME for Clotel. She was coming, had been coming. Even before the girl was born, Zena had passed through Venita's dreams. There in the garden, all those years ago, hidden under the hardness of the earth, under the darkness of the night, she snatched the child away.

Zena showed up on a night of cold rain in the late spring of 1976. It had been nearly a year since she left.

Venita would have liked to say the knock at her front door sounded different. She would have liked to think this scene would be tragic, dramatic, that she would swoon in Moses's arms and he would revive her by gently patting her face and sprinkling water on her. A small baptism. She would have liked to see herself and Moses gnashing their teeth at the Lord. Oh, what had they done to deserve this?

But Moses was asleep when Zena came, and so was Clotel. All Zena said was, "I understand you got my baby. I come for her." Her breath was sweet, like mint.

"Come in," Venita said. "She upstairs. I'll go get her."

Walking on numb feet, Zena's sweet breath caught up in her nose, Venita slowly ascended the stairs, woke Moses up, and told him Zena was downstairs. Moses did not say anything, and would not even get out of bed. So Venita went into Clotel's room, turned on the light, and packed her things. She refused to let herself look at Clotel.

Not long after she and Moses had taken Clotel in, Mary Kate told Venita, "Maybe ya'll should bring her downtown, get something done legal, so if her mama come back, she can't take her."

"I ain't going downtown messing with no white people. They might take her."

"They won't take her. You and Moses good people. Why would they take her?"

"This don't sound like you, Kate," Venita said.

"Mikey the one that said it," Mary Kate said, and added softly, "I know the boy don't make no sense sometime, but what he say got some truth in it, and you know time coming up for her to go to school."

"We going to send her."

Mary Kate dropped the subject. She and Venita both knew that a girl as young and fickle as Zena, who would take off so suddenly, could just as suddenly reappear.

Venita had rehearsed the scene, had written the entire play, so when the time came she would be ready, believing in the absurd notion that if you rehearsed for tragedy, you were better prepared to face it.

When her father had died back in '65, when she had received the call from her Aunt Hattie, she thought then she would be ready. The buying of the black dress, the long bus ride home, the knowing her father was dead, did not prepare her for seeing him in a small coffin, his face gray, his stiff hands clenched around a Bible, a book he never read, since he could not read. Though she had thought herself ready, she still expected to see him with a drink in his hand, and when he was buried, she had wailed with the rest of the women.

Sorrow has a finite depth, breadth, width. Venita knew this, for she had woven hers into a cloak and hidden behind it. Sorrow could not touch her as she looked at the child who had come and broken the silence in her life with Moses.

It was not as if Clotel had done anything, said any one thing to change their lives, for she was a quiet child. It was the sight of her combing a doll's hair, the feel of her hand in theirs, the sound of her walking upstairs over their heads, the sound of her breath while she slept.

The first time Moses and Venita heard her laugh, they were in bed on a cold Saturday morning, deciding if they should make love, if they had time before Clotel woke up. Having to decide added secrecy and intimacy to their lives, which they had not had since they were teens and made love in the far corner of Venita's parents' garden the summer before Moses went north. He would wait impatiently for her in the night, calling like an owl from the woods. They would lie with his shirt bunched under her head, their eyes closed, their ears open to any sound rising from the green and soft earth.

On that Saturday morning, as she and Moses lay together, the girl's laughter rose, eddying and curling around the banister, every bit as shocking as the smell of smoke. They left the bed quietly and walked halfway down the stairs, to see Clotel and her doll sitting less than a foot away from the television, watching cartoons.

Like anyone who retreats into a world of dreams, Clotel would awake in the night, blinded by the blackness of her room, and think she was still sleeping, lying in a dreamless void, waiting to be awakened. Dreams now passed her by on their way to children who needed them more than she.

She slept less, entered more into the world of wakefulness, and began stumbling through the house, breaking things. The first thing she broke was an ashtray Venita had gotten in Atlantic City. She bumped into the cocktail table, and the dish shattered on the floor. Clotel ran and hid in the closet under the stairs, expecting to be beaten. She refused to come out for hours, even when Moses came home from work. Not until after dinner did she emerge, her eyes puffy, her face flushed. She was not beaten. She was given her dinner. Moses and Venita were never angry with her, even when she dropped her fork, spilled a glass of milk, splashed water from the tub. Zena would fly into a rage over offenses smaller than these. Once she had beaten Clotel because she had forgotten to flush the toilet.

Clotel never asked where her mother was, why she had gone, but to Venita it seemed the child's restless, searching eyes were watching out for Zena. Her mother had told her that her protruding blue eyes made her look ugly, like a fish, and Clotel had come to feel that way, submerged in the blueness of her house, as colorless as a creature on the floor of the deepest of oceans, unexposed to light, living under atmospheres of pressure.

But in this new house life drifted down to her.

Before school started, the Taylor girls Jonetta and Olivia came over to Venita's to play with her. This was beyond her experience. The knock on the door was for her. Someone had come to see her. She went out with them and watched them play hand-clapping games, singing all those names she had heard ringing through All-Bright Court so many times: Miss Mary Mack, Miss Sue, the pretty little Dutch girl, Punchinello.

When they sang Sally Walker, they gyrated their hips and shook their shoulders, urging on the weeping Sally sitting in the middle of the circle:

> Rise, Sally, Rise.
> Wipe them tears out eyes.
> Put your hands on hips,
> And let your backbone slip.
> Ah, shake it to the east,
> Ah, shake it to the west,
> Ah, shake it to the very one you like the best
> Sally West.

Clotel liked this game. There was no falling down, not like ring around the rosie, when the girls turned themselves into piles of ashes. Here was only a rising up as the girls danced and shook their troubles away.

It was not until the spring that Clotel entered the game, when Jonetta picked her to come into the center.

And there, in the brief and late spring, Clotel rose from the ground that still held winter. The earth was yet to give way to the softness, the gentle push of warmth, sun, rain. It did not yield when Clotel began shaking as if in a trance, her hands on her hips, her head thrown back, her white face turned up to the sun. She shook to the east and west. When the girls stopped singing, she kept on dancing, shaking to the north, to the south, and all the girls stood around watching.

One finally said, "Stop, girl, and pick somebody."

Clotel did not stop. She kept on dancing until Jonetta jumped into the center and grabbed her by the shoulders. Clotel stopped and stood squinting at the blueness of the sky, waiting for rain to chase her back into hiding. None fell, and still looking upward, she walked from the center of the circle.

Venita could not put off looking at Clotel any longer. It was time to wake her. She sat on the bed next to the child, who was curled up on her side like a baby.

Below the lids, Clotel's eyes were moving rapidly. Venita called to her, but she would not respond. She shook the child, and when this did not wake her, she tried to lift her. But she was so heavy in sleep that Venita could not move her.

She went to get Moses to take the child down. But he could not face Clotel to say goodbye.

"That woman waiting now," Venita pleaded. "Get on up." Moses would rather have stayed in bed, his face to the wall, but he got up and walked past Venita into Clotel's room.

Venita followed. Clotel lay more tightly curled than before, and when Moses went to lift her, it seemed as if she had fastened herself to the bed. When he finally got her up, she went limp in his arms. Venita picked up her things, and they descended the stairs. It was as though they were being summarily dismissed, given back their unadorned life. And they were going to go back without a fight, back into an existence that was as white and slick as the inside of an eggshell, into a seamless life that curved around itself, defining its own scope. Even before the rising of the sun, Venita would be up cooking Moses breakfast, packing him a lunch. Moses would go to work, and when he returned Venita would have his dinner ready. Later, when neither could avoid it any longer, they would drift upstairs, and though they would sleep in the same bed, they would be at opposite ends of an open field, he calling to her like an owl, she no longer able to hear him.

Zena was sitting, smoking, flicking ashes into a cut-glass candy dish. She took a few more drags before she put the cigarette out, and she stood up.

"This all her stuff?" Zena asked, taking the things from Venita and moving toward the door.

"I'll carry her to where ya'll going," Moses offered.

"I got a car outside, and you can put her down. She ain't even sleep," Zena said. "You ain't even sleep," she said to Clotel. "Get up."

The child stiffened in Moses's arms, and then her legs arched downward as she made an effort to stand. Moses placed her on her feet.

"Let's go," Zena said to her, taking her by the hand. Clotel began walking, her eyes closed. There was no need to open them, for she would still be in bed, still dreaming.

"Wait," Venita said. "I forgot her doll, and her coat. She shouldn't go out without a coat. I'm a run up and get them."

"Don't trouble yourself. She be all right. She ain't going to need a coat. We going to California," Zena said, her smoky breath in Venita's face.

Zena led Clotel out the door, and Clotel kept her roving eyes shut tight, even as the rain began to fall.

25

WHERE'S JOE?

MIKEY had sulked when he found out his father did not have the money to send him on his class trip. Over the spring break, the class was going to Washington, D.C., to celebrate the bicentennial year. Mikey did not dare tell anyone at school that he could not go because of money. He simply said his family had made other plans. His friend Scott wasn't going either. He and some of his friends were driving to Florida. Mikey didn't understand why his father didn't have the money. He did not know that his father had been a slave for four years now.

"We have been sold into slavery!" the local representative screamed at the rank and file gathered in the union hall. It was two weeks before Christmas. Nixon had been reelected. The men, still dazed by the layoffs that had come earlier that year, sat tired and confused. In the back of the room was a line of men. Samuel stood in the line. The hall was not even full, but there were not enough seats. At a meeting the previous week, half of the wooden folding chairs had been destroyed.

The men had been called in to view a film, *Where's Joe?*
Joe was an American steelworker without a job. Joe had not
worked hard enough. He had wanted too much money, too
many benefits. Joe was on the unemployment line.

"Where's Hans?" the film asked. "Where's Oda?"

Hans and Oda had Joe's job. They had worked harder.
They had worked longer, for lower wages. They had sacri-
ficed for the good of their nations.

Finally, the film posed the question "Will you be Joe?"
The men had grumbled through the movie, but when the
final question was asked, a chair winged through the air, its
seat flapping shut, and knocked down the pull-up screen.
The men began smashing chairs. They tore the reel from the
projector and ripped apart the film, as if Oda and Hans
were inside it, living in one of the frames, as if their union
president, Petrovich, could be strangled by twisting the film.

If only they could get their hands on Petrovich, they
would tear his lame-duck wings from his body. After the
men had been laid off, without the consent, advice, or even
knowledge of the rank and file, Petrovich had met with management and signed their lives away. He had taken away
their right to strike.

The agreement he signed was called the ENA, the Experi-
mental Negotiating Agreement. It would be a way of protecting the men, to keep foreign steel from taking advantage
of domestic steel. If there was to be a strike, the Germans or
Japanese could make inroads by selling their product more
cheaply. Strikes were not only obsolete, they were dangerous. Whether or not the men agreed, their amended contract
was binding.

Samuel focused his attention on the representative at the
podium. "Let me read something to you," the man said.
"This is a quote, now, not my words. 'I'd like to see democ-

racy exercised to the fullest extent in our union or any other union, but democracy in the labor movement, as in various segments of life, can be carried too far.'

"I probably don't even have to tell you who said that. It was Petrovich, the lousy son of a bitch, lame duck. Too much democracy! That's what he's saying. Where the hell does he think we are, Russia? Petrovich is Russian. You know what I'm saying? You *know* what I'm saying. He's trying to sell us into slavery, the stinking Red."

Samuel did not know if Petrovich was a Red. He did know he was a redneck.

During the fall of that year Gerald Thompson, a black staff representative, won a nomination as a candidate for international vice president. The then vice president was retiring. Despite the fact Thompson was backed by the black members of the U.A.W., who numbered one third of the union's membership, Petrovich invalidated the nomination. It came to his attention that in 1965, while Thompson was hospitalized with a work-related injury, he had let his dues lapse.

"We will fight, fight, fight!" the union representative yelled. "We have a contract that doesn't say we can't strike. We're going to court because that agreement Petrovich made isn't right and it isn't legal."

Before the rank and file went to negotiate its new contract, a ruling was handed down on the no-strike policy. The judge hearing the case said, "In any system of self-government, in theory and in practice even the most precious of rights may be waived, assuming that the system established for making such a decision is followed."

Because the rank and file had voted Petrovich in, what he did might not have been right, but it was legal. The no-strike policy would be in effect until 1977.

Work or leave. Those were the choices the men faced. How could that be considered slavery? No one forced into involuntary servitude had the option of leaving.

When the contract came back, there was a twenty-eight-cent-an-hour raise the first year, and sixteen cents for each of the next two years. In just fourteen years, steelworkers dropped from first to fourteenth on the wage scale of industrial workers.

The men worked while management continued streamlining the industry, combining and eliminating jobs and starting a "speed-up" campaign. There was no featherbedding. And the men's loyalty to the 1974 contract was rewarded. Each worker was given a flat one-hundred-fifty-dollar bonus. Management had no hard feelings.

In the bicentennial year, when sixty-five thousand domestic specialty-steel jobs were threatened by imports from Germany and Japan, Samuel knew Hans and Oda were working, and he was glad to be working, even with emphysema. He was glad he was not Joe.

Mikey would not be making the trip, but he was leaving anyway. He was going to graduate the next year, a full year early, and he was going east. Every school he was applying to was in New England.

"Why don't you apply to some college 'round here? They got some good schools in Buffalo," Mary Kate had said to Mikey one day while he was preparing to go out on his route.

"Mama, there are no good schools around here. I'm not going to go to a state university. I can get into the Ivy League."

Samuel asked, "What's that?"

"Dad," Mikey said, "everyone knows what the Ivy League is."

"I don't," Samuel said. "Your mama don't know neither."

"They're the best colleges in the country, the world!" Mikey said.

"If you want to go away to school, you should think 'bout going to a black college, someplace like Southern," Mary Kate said.

"Southern?" Samuel asked.

Mary Kate said, "Yeah, it's a fine school, and then there's Grambling, Howard —"

"I'm not going to any black college," Mikey said, folding the last of his papers.

"He right. He ain't going to one of them," Samuel said, coughing. "If he want to get what the white man got, he better go where the white man go."

Mikey left with his papers.

That night, when Mary Kate and Samuel were in bed, she asked, "Why you tell Mikey what you did?"

"What?" he asked. He had been half asleep, his back to her.

"You not wanting him to go to a black college."

"Kate, could you see him at one?"

"Well, I can't see where he want to go. He just want to get away from us." Her voice was thin, brittle.

Samuel turned to face her. In a wheezing voice he said, "That ain't true. Don't you think that."

"It is true. I worry 'bout him more than any of our children. Him graduating early, he doing that so he can get away. He going to be lost to us," she said, her voice cracking.

"Hush, now," Samuel said, his words floating into the shadows of the room. "He going to be all right. Let me tell you something," he said, reaching out for his wife in the darkness. "He going to be a blessing to us in our old age."

26

SNOWBOUND

FOR JUST a minute Mikey was lost. Only a few blocks from home, he could have been in a desert, swept up in a simoom, sand becoming sky, becoming air, blinding him, choking him.

But he was on Ridge Road, caught out in the worst storm of the century, the blizzard of '77. Mikey wished the storm was something he had dreamed up. If he were dreaming, someone would come and wake him, and he would find himself safely in bed. He would settle for seeing Isaac, welcome his haunting presence. Isaac could scare him out of this nightmare.

As Mikey had gotten off the bus, the driver had said, "I hope you're close to home. The way it's coming down, you might never get there."

Only then did it occur to Mikey that he might be in danger. Though it took him five hours to get to Lackawanna, though the two buses he had to take had been late, had stopped and skidded and lumbered along through snow fall-

ing at a rate of two inches an hour, though along the lakefront there had been zero visibility and the driver nearly hit
seven abandoned cars, Mikey had not let himself believe the
storm could harm him.

The storm was not unexpected. High winds and ten
inches to a foot of snow had been predicted. The flurries had
begun early that morning, a little snow slipping in unobtru-
sively over the lake.

The headmaster at Essex had decided at ten in the morning there would be a full day of classes. Then it had been
snowing steadily, but not heavily. The previous week he had
dismissed classes at noon because a heavy snowfall had been
predicted. But less than an inch fell, leaving smokelike spi-
rals of snow dancing across the deserted campus, and the
headmaster looked foolish. He was not going to repeat that
mistake.

As Mikey had sat in his last class of the day, watching as
the world was being obliterated by whiteness, he thought
that back in All-Bright Court everyone must surely be thinking that the world was ending, that this storm was a plague
being visited upon them by God.

His mother had phoned twice. Before he had left school
at the end of the day, Mikey had taken down two pink mes-
sage slips tacked to the bulletin board outside the headmaster's office and stuffed them in one of his books. He knew
how worried his mother must be, but he was not going to
feed her irrational fears by calling.

Scott had offered to let him stay at his house. It wasn't far
from the school, but Mikey had declined. He would show
his parents that he was more than capable of taking care of
himself.

But when he had gotten off the bus from Buffalo, when
the bus had been swallowed by the night and the storm, its

red taillights moving steadily away, he began to feel frightened. In that instant he had become disoriented, turned around, unsure of the way.

It was then that he fell. His books scattered, disappearing into the snow. His papers blew from his books, flapping their way skyward.

Mikey lay there a few moments, stunned, the snow enveloping him in a nebulous, cold whiteness. He knew that if he did not get up he would die. He tried to struggle to his feet, but the wind was too strong, the snow falling too heavily. He thought this was how it would be. Him alone. Lost.

After several more minutes he managed to get on his hands and knees. He was out of breath. Snow had gotten down his collar, up his sleeves, in his pant legs, soaking him through. Its coldness was deceiving. It felt like fire. He could not trust his senses. As he turned to face what might be the direction of home, he thought he saw a figure advancing steadily toward him, pressing against the storm.

Again he thought he was in a dream and this was Isaac coming for him, even though he knew Isaac was safely locked away.

The figured loomed closer, no more than a shadow, no more than a ghost, until it stood over him. It was his father.

Samuel helped his son up from the ground. He was saying something to Mikey, but Mikey could not hear a word. The wind was reaching into his father's mouth, snatching his words away, sending them flying into oblivion.